"You think you can handle me touching you in public?" he whispered.

"Kissing you. Acting like I'm your lover and pretending to know every single detail about your body?"

Jenna's breath caught in her throat. "I bet you that I can fool anyone who looks at us," she told Mac, trying to catch her breath. "So long as everyone thinks we're an item, that's all I care about."

"I've never turned down a bet." He continued to stroke her skin. Her collarbone, her jaw, the sensitive spot behind her ear. "What does the winner get?"

Jenna swallowed, forcing herself to focus. "If we pull this off, I win and you'll owe me another favor, which I can redeem at any time."

His brow quirked up. "And if I win?"

"You won't. I plan to be very convincing."

Mac's warm breath tickled her cheek as he shifted. One palm slid up the side of her face, his fingers threading into her hair. "Then we'd better practice."

* * *

From Friend to Fake Fiancé is part of the Mafia Moguls series: for this tight-knit mob family, going legitimate leads to love!

Dear Reader,

When I started the Mafia Moguls series, I knew I wanted a friends-to-lovers trope—one of my absolute favorite storylines. So, who better to use than jet-setting playboy Mac O'Shea? You may recall him from book one, *Trapped with the Tycoon*. Mac may have had the hots for his friend for years, but he's been hands off, respecting their special bond.

Jenna LeBlanc needs a fake boyfriend and trusts no one other than her BFF. Oh, I had to throw in an exotic setting and a wedding, just to amp up the tension between this dynamic couple. You're welcome!

This story was so much fun to work on. Procrastinating... er, researching Bora Bora on Pinterest has made me want to get my passport out and pack a bag! I hope you enjoy the second story in this series and keep your eyes open for the next. I promise, there are more surprises revealed in each book. You won't want to miss a moment of these bad boys from Boston!

Happy reading,

Jules

JULES BENNETT

———

FROM FRIEND TO FAKE FIANCÉ

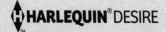

ISBN-13: 978-0-373-73460-3

From Friend to Fake Fiancé

Copyright © 2016 by Jules Bennett

www.Harlequin.com

Award-winning author **Jules Bennett** is no stranger to romance—she met her husband when she was only fourteen. After dating through high school, the two married. He encouraged her to chase her dream of becoming an author. Jules has now published nearly thirty novels. She and her husband are living their own happily-ever-after while raising two girls. Jules loves to hear from readers through her website, julesbennett.com, her Facebook fan page or on Twitter.

Books by Jules Bennett

HARLEQUIN DESIRE

What the Prince Wants
A Royal Amnesia Scandal
Maid for a Magnate

The Barrington Trilogy

When Opposites Attract...
Single Man Meets Single Mom
Carrying the Lost Heir's Child

Mafia Moguls

Trapped with the Tycoon
From Friend to Fake Fiancé

HARLEQUIN SPECIAL EDITION

The St. Johns of Stonerock

Dr. Daddy's Perfect Christmas
The Fireman's Ready-Made Family
From Best Friend to Bride

Visit her Author Profile page at Harlequin.com, or julesbennett.com, for more titles.

There's no greater happily-ever-after than sharing the journey with your best friend. Love you, Michael.

One

"All I need you to do is play the part of my boyfriend for the next week."

"Let me get this straight. You had me fly to Bora Bora so we can make your ex believe you've moved on. We'll be pretending to shack up in this romantic hut. And in the midst of all of that, you'll be doing the flowers for your sister's wedding?"

Okay, when Mac O'Shea phrased the question like that, the situation did sound rather ridiculous. But she had her reasons, damn it. Good reasons. Reasons that justified making her very best friend pose as her boyfriend.

Standing in the cozy hut that was her home for the next week, Jenna LeBlanc adjusted the strap on her favorite coral sundress and stared at Mac. "Listen, you love to travel and I'm giving you a free trip. Stop complaining."

Shoving his suitcase out of the way with the toe of his shoe, Mac stalked toward her. Emerald eyes held her in her place, as if daring her to move until he got to the bottom of this. Mercy, that man was potent. Her best friend was sexier than any other man she'd ever encountered and now she needed him to pretend to be madly in love with her because she trusted nobody else. Sure. This should be no problem.

"I can afford my own damn trip." He propped his hands on his hips as he stopped right before her. "I want to know why you didn't tell me the full reason you needed me down here when you called."

Humiliation? Fear? Too many emotions swirled around, leaving her more desperate than she'd like to be. The need to keep her sister's wedding perfect and her mother's past demons from creeping up had Jenna putting everything on the line. Heart, sanity…everything.

"Listen, Martin is still attending because he's the best man," she explained. "We broke up two weeks ago and he wants me back. He won't take no for an answer. There's no way to avoid him here, so that's where you come in."

Mac's dark brows drew in as the muscle ticked in his square jaw. "You told me you broke things off with him, but you never said why."

"Well, you were gallivanting around the world—"

"In Barcelona."

"And you didn't return my call when I tried to reach you."

"Because I was in a meeting when you called and your message said to come here." Mac sighed. "Now, tell me what the hell is going on and why we're dating, because if we are, my family needs to know. My sister will be thrilled."

Jenna narrowed her eyes. "Now is not the time to be snarky."

Mac crossed his arms over his massive, broad, extremely chiseled chest. She couldn't help but stare as the material strained across his shoulders. They may be only friends, but that never stopped her from eyeing the goods. Mac made thirty-two look damn sexy.

"Martin was screwing his assistant."

It hurt to say those words. Not because she'd been madly in love with him; they'd only been dating a few months. But to know he didn't feel she was worthy enough for him to break up with first? Did men not consider women's feelings anymore?

"He was a jerk anyway," Mac commented. "Want me to rough him up?"

She laughed, though she knew he wasn't kidding entirely. Rumors of the O'Sheas' infamous ways of conducting "business" were strong enough that his words rang true. Mac's father, Patrick, had passed away less than a year ago and the man wasn't known for his gentle hand or kind mannerisms. Mac's brother Braden had taken over as head of the family, and he and his fiancée, Zara, were much more personable, but Braden was still a formidable presence. He wasn't a man to mess with, either, but had more tact, self-control—and quite possibly more power—than Patrick did.

"Seeing Martin in pain would be lovely, but no thanks." Jenna patted his cheek and went on. "But since he has to be here, I refuse to have him believe I am available. As far as he's concerned, I've moved on and I'm head over heels for you. He's nothing but a bad memory."

"And this is where my undying love comes in."

Jenna swallowed hard. "If you want to put it that way, then, yes. But I really just need a favor without the sarcastic comments."

Jenna didn't want to think of Mac and love in the same sentence. That would be a cruel trick to play on herself.

Yes, they'd been best friends since he tried to pick her up years ago at the party of a mutual friend. She'd blown him off, thinking there was no way a guy like that would ever find her attractive. Added to that, she'd been in Boston long enough to know the O'Shea name and hadn't wanted to associate herself with people who were synonymous with "mafia" and "mob."

Apparently he'd found her bold rejection appealing because he'd pursued her anyway. She'd told him she was a long-term type of girl, and he'd said he admired that but he wasn't in the market for a relationship. Now she laughed at the fact that they were indeed long-term, but as friends only.

Jenna had to admit, he was like no other friend she'd ever had. She'd seen a side to him that didn't seem ruthless or conniving at all. He made her laugh, made her relax. She didn't know when the switch occurred, but one day she knew who her best friend was and that he would do anything for her. And his friendship wasn't a bad connection to have. Mac wasn't just a jet-setting playboy, his family owned auction houses around the globe, brought in billions each year and were a force to be reckoned with in the international business world.

Yet, after all these years of knowing him, she still wasn't sure which side of the law the family truly operated on. Jenna had brought that topic up only one time in the past decade—a mistake she wouldn't make again. She'd asked about his family business, why all the traveling and secrecy. Mac had turned almost cold and made it perfectly clear that topic was off limits and not to be approached ever again. Which is why she wasn't asking about the Barcelona trip or the meeting he'd been in.

Mac stared at her for a moment, then hitched his hip onto the bamboo-and-wicker barstool at the island in the kitchen of her bungalow. "If your sister isn't getting married for another week, why are we here now?"

Because her perfect sister wanted the perfect wedding to go along with her perfect life. Jenna loved her sister more than anything, but Amy seriously had it all. Jenna had…no. She wasn't going to start down that path because she was happy for her sister and that's why she was here. Jenna didn't want to be the bitter bridesmaid simply because she had a cheating ex. Amy had actually found true love and this was going to be the best week of her life. She deserved perfect.

Jenna hadn't told her family why she and Martin parted ways. A fake boyfriend would really go a long way to keep everyone all smiles until this wedding was over.

"Amy wants her wedding party and guests to enjoy the island. Kind of a mini-vacation for them and a giant party building up to the main event."

When Mac didn't say anything, Jenna sighed and tugged the top of her dress up another inch. Damn boobs. These little sundresses always looked so good on those plastic, size two models but were hard to pull off in reality.

"You don't have to. I know it's silly and desperate and ridiculous to ask—"

"What would you expect of me?" he asked, a naughty smile spreading across his face. "And don't skimp on the details."

Letting out an unladylike growl, Jenna rolled her eyes and marched through the luxurious hut and straight out the door leading to a small, straw-covered deck overlooking the crystal-blue water. Heavy footsteps sounded behind her and seconds later a familiar, firm hand settled over her shoulder.

"I'm not in the mood to be made fun of."

With a gentle squeeze, Mac turned her around. "Fine. Tell me what you need me to do."

She stared up into the emerald eyes she'd found herself getting lost in more than once. "You'll have to stay in this hut with me."

"Done."

She swallowed. "There's only one bedroom."

His mouth quirked up. "Then try to keep your hands to yourself."

"Can you focus?"

Jenna couldn't help but laugh. He flirted with any woman between eighteen and death. He had no filter and she never took him seriously. The man loved life, loved women and loved his family. He was loyal to a fault. If she thought for even a second he could do long term, she could fall so easily for him. But she kept her heart guarded and firmly planted on the friendship side.

"I'm focused," he insisted, holding his hands out. "One bedroom. I understand what we won't be doing in there, so tell me what we'll be doing outside our little house."

"You'll need to come to the evening events with me. There are only a few." Jenna ran the list down in her head. "I'm doing all the flowers for the ceremony, so if you could make some trips with me to assist with the arrangements, that would look all boyfriend-ish. Oh, there's the rehearsal dinner and ceremony, too, of course. But during the day, we may need to be seen on the beach together holding hands. I don't know…doing lovey-dovey things."

"Lovey-dovey? Whatever you mean by that, I can handle it." He glanced out at the water for a second, then back to her. "There's only one problem."

Her heart sank. She didn't have time for problems. Her mom was arriving in the morning and who knew when her ex would show his cheater face. Stupid guy had to be the best man, which meant she'd be walking down the aisle with him…she'd rather walk barefoot on broken glass.

"I've known you for ten years and you're not the affectionate type."

Jenna swallowed and nodded in agreement. There was a reason she wasn't all touchy-feely. She couldn't afford to be.

"I can be," she assured him.

"Really?" He took a step forward, instantly filling the gap between them.

His hand came up to her face as he trailed his fingertips down her cheek, to her jawline and down her neck. She couldn't suppress the tremble that racked her body.

"You think you can handle me touching you in public?" he whispered. "Kissing you? Acting like I'm your lover and pretending to know every single detail about your body?"

Jenna's breath caught in her throat. The idea of Mac knowing every inch of her body both thrilled and terrified her. She had no doubt this man knew how to bring pleasure, but at the same time, she'd be mortified if he saw her naked and looked disappointed. Her body wasn't perfect, far from it. The curves, the dips and rolls, everything about her physique was the exact opposite of the women she'd seen him with.

"I bet you that I can fool anyone who sees us," she told him, trying to catch her breath. "So long as Martin thinks we're an item, that's all I care about."

"I've never turned down a bet." He continued to stroke her skin. Her collarbone, her jaw, the sensitive spot behind her ear. "What does the winner get?"

Jenna swallowed, forcing herself to focus. "If we pull

this off, I win and you'll owe me another favor, which I can redeem at any time."

His brow quirked up. "And if I win?"

"You won't. I plan on being very convincing."

Mac's warm breath tickled her cheek as she shifted under his touch. He slid one palm up the side of her face, his fingers threading through her hair. "Then we better practice before he arrives."

Before she could ask what he meant, his mouth claimed hers.

What. The. Hell?

Mac's question to his own sanity quickly evaporated the second Jenna opened to him. He swallowed her gasp and kept his hand firm on her jaw, as if daring her to pull away.

Finally, after all these years of wondering how his best friend would taste, now he knew and the fantasy didn't even come close to touching reality. And he'd had a multitude of fantasies regarding this stunning woman.

Jenna stiffened against him, then melted. There was no other word for what happened with her body— those curves would be the death of him.

For years he'd kept his distance out of respect to their friendship and because there was no way in hell he'd let her in deeper...not when his family had secrets he could never share. His father had been a killer, though Patrick O'Shea could justify each and every death. Mac had actually made the decision himself twice before, when Braden wouldn't do it and Patrick was forcing their hand. Mac didn't look back, though. No regrets. Regrets meant living in the past. His family was looking toward the future, looking to go legit. The idea seemed so simple, but the execution—no pun intended—was proving to be a bit harder to pull off.

Mac's family was cunning; they got what they wanted. They stole, lied and would betray anyone to get where they needed to be. On the flip side, the O'Sheas were fiercely loyal to their allies. They wouldn't hesitate to help anyone legitimately in need. But pity those foolish enough to cross them.

There were so many family secrets, Mac knew full well he'd never put a woman he loved in a position of having to lie to the cops or keep the darkness of their deeds hidden.

For the most part, the O'Sheas put up a great front. Yet beneath the surface they were always watching, waiting, ready to strike at any threat to their family.

Braden had found love, but Mac wasn't so sure such a thing existed for him. He didn't do relationships. Jenna was a relationship type of girl, so friends was all they could ever be. Because he wasn't letting her out of his life. She got him. She knew his family was…unique, and she didn't pry.

But playing boyfriend to her for a week? Now that he could totally get behind. The green light to touch her, to kiss her, was the stuff of fantasies and he planned on making every second count. Because if he was going to play this role, he intended to take it all the way. He hoped like hell she knew what she was getting into.

After their little charade was over, she'd be out of his system and they could go back to being friends. He'd pushed for more years ago, but she'd shut him down, stating she was only looking for something long term. Now she'd made the first move and all he had to do was follow her orders…and touching Jenna after all this time would be one benefit he'd never forget.

And when the ex showed up, Mac planned on having a little one-on-one chat with the bastard. Nobody hurt Jenna and lived to tell about it. And no one made her feel less about herself. She was a beautiful, vibrant woman deserving of a man who would appreciate her.

And for a week, Mac would be that man…in theory.

Mac tipped his head, rubbing his lips against Jenna's before capturing her mouth once again. Her fingertips curled into his shirt as he slid his hands down that sultry, killer body. If he was going to pretend to be her boyfriend, he wanted all the perks that came with it.

"Oh. I'm sorry!"

Jenna jerked in his arms. Mac didn't let her go as he glanced toward the doorway where Jenna's mother and sister stood. They were clearly embarrassed, seeing as how neither of them were making eye contact. Mac didn't care that they were seen during a very private moment, he actually found it rather amusing.

Besides, getting caught in the act was something he'd grown used to over the years, considering his family's activities. Thankfully, with the right law enforcement and powerful people in his family's back pocket, he'd never been arrested or faced charges.

When Jenna started to shift away, Mac tightened his grip. Might as well practice now, if they were going to pull this charade off for the ex. If they could make her mother and sister believe, then the ex would be no problem whatsoever. And after this week they could simply tell Mary and Amy that he and Jenna had decided they were better off as friends. An easy fix and they'd both still get everything they wanted: Jenna would get her ex to stay away and Mac would get her in his bed.

"We didn't mean to…"

"I had no idea you two…"

Mary and Amy spoke at the same time and Mac laughed. "You're fine. I just arrived myself and I was giving Jenna a proper hello."

Mary's eyes widened as she stared at her daughter. "You just broke up with Martin two weeks ago."

Jenna remained frozen at his side and he knew she was struggling with how to explain this scenario to her family. Coming to her defense was easy.

"Martin is an ass," Mac stated. "Jenna and I have danced around our attraction for years and we thought spending some time here away from work and reality would help us figure out if we should take things to the next level."

"What are you two doing here?" Jenna croaked out.

Mary nodded. "I thought we could get some girl time in before the guests started arriving. I didn't know you'd already had company, but I'm glad Mac is with you. Martin was a nice guy, but Mac is…well, you know I love him."

Mary smiled and Mac knew he had them fooled. These three women were strong, united and had a bond that rivaled that of his own family. He hated lying to Jenna's family. But it was necessary and nothing he and Jenna couldn't get out of later.

Amy let out a little squeal as she stepped forward and wrapped her arms around Jenna, spinning her in a circle. "I knew you two would end up together. I'm so happy for you guys. I'm sorry Martin is the best man and you have to walk with him, but I promise you and Mac will have an amazing time."

Jenna glared at Mac over her sister's shoulder and he knew he'd crossed the line. He was going to have some explaining to do once they were alone.

He sent her a wink and a grin, which only earned him a narrowed gaze. Oh, yeah. This boyfriend scenario was going to be fun.

Two

"What the hell was all of that?"

Okay, he'd expected her to be pissed. He'd kissed her, lied to her family and then she'd had time to stew about everything once her mother and sister had whisked her away for a family dinner. The ladies' dinner conversation was a no-brainer. He had no doubt Jenna had been bombarded with questions that she likely didn't have answers to all because of that kiss.

He wasn't sorry.

Mac quirked a brow, knowing his silent action would get under her skin. It was just too easy to push her buttons… and she was sexy as hell all fired up like this.

Throwing her arms in the air, Jenna growled and slammed the door to their hut. "Do you have any idea what I just had to endure, all because you couldn't keep your lips and hands to yourself?"

So what? She had to discuss the kiss with her sister

and mother. He'd had to sit here in the silence and replay it over and over in his head. He could still taste her if he licked his lips, could still feel her when he clenched his fists.

"Are you going to say anything?"

"Did you bring me anything to eat?" he asked. "I'm starving."

She crossed the room in two strides and shoved at his chest. "My mother wants to know how serious we are and my sister is already making plans for a double date with her fiancé and us. Are you ready for this?"

Mac wouldn't be pushed, literally or figuratively, by anyone—even his best friend. He gripped her wrists, tugging on her until she fell against him. Perfect.

"You got this ball rolling, I only gave it an extra nudge. If you want your ex to believe we're lovers, then practicing on your family is the perfect place to start."

Jenna stared into his eyes. "I don't like lying to them."

"We're not lying. I fully intend to take you for my lover."

Her body stilled against his, her eyes widened. "Wh-what?"

"You heard me." He was confident the shock in her eyes only masked her desire. She'd kissed him with too much passion, had practically melted against him. No way could he ignore her response. "I plan on fully experiencing being your lover, and when the week is over we'll go back to being friends. That way nobody will be lying to your family."

She jerked away from him, raking her shaky hands through her hair. She twisted it up into a knot and closed her eyes. Mac crossed his arms while he waited for her to process the kink he'd just put into her plans.

With a sigh, she dropped her arms and her hair fell all

around her shoulders in messy waves. "We aren't sleeping together. I need a friend, Mac. I take sex seriously. I know you can detach yourself from the emotions that come with intimacy, but I can't."

Knowing he was on shaky ground here, Mac closed the gap between them until he was so near she had to tip her head to look up at him. Her face was totally devoid of makeup, yet the tan she'd gotten was all the glow she needed to be even more radiant. Women he dated tended to use spackling to enhance their beauty, but Jenna needed nothing extra. He preferred a woman who wasn't all made up in an attempt to gain attention.

"I know you want long term, Jenna. But this week is all about special circumstances. You invited me here." He purposely used a softer tone. "Let's see where this goes. I promise, when this is over we'll go back to being friends. Nobody will get hurt, Jenna."

"Says the man who has women strewn throughout the world."

He suppressed a smile. "Despite what you think of my travels, most of the time it's business and I'm too damn tired to entertain."

She shook her head and took another step back, hitting the wall by the front door. "Sex implies…"

He quirked a brow. "Lust, desire, passion? I'm willing to admit you're hot and any man would be lucky to have you in his bed."

She put her hands on his chest. When she didn't push him away, he reached out, curling his fingers around her bare shoulders.

"Don't," she warned. "We're not sleeping together. We're not doing anything but pretending to be lovers. After this week, my family will think we just decided to stay friends. That's all. I can't do more and if you're honest with yourself, you can't, either."

Oh, he could do plenty more. Starting with peeling that dress from her curvy body. But he wouldn't push her. She was already feeling stressed and recovering from the betrayal of her asshat ex. The last thing she needed was for her best friend to force her into anything. But that didn't mean he would stop his attempts to get her into his bed. For years he'd wondered how it would feel to have his best friend in every way possible and now he had this week to seduce her. Bora Bora provided the perfect backdrop for temptation, with its sultry nights and lazy days on the beach. Seducing Jenna would be so easy, so perfect. Before these seven days were up, he'd know exactly how amazing they were together.

But Mac didn't want her to feel forced, to feel pressured. He wanted her willing and aching for him. He wanted her to admit that the attraction was mutual. There wasn't a doubt in his mind she wanted him. She may be lying to herself, but her actions spoke volumes.

Stroking his thumbs along her delicate skin, Mac bent slightly to hold her gaze. "I'm not putting any pressure on you. You've got enough going on now."

Beneath his palms, her shoulders relaxed. "I still have all those flowers to do and Amy has changed her mind about the arrangements twice already. My ex will be showing up any day and I'm exhausted from my mother's questions. If you add more stress on me, I'm going to smother you in your sleep."

Laughing, Mac pulled her in and wrapped his arms around her. She literally fell against his chest as if the fight had gone out of her. This would be the perfect opportunity to seduce her…if he wanted to be a complete, uncaring jerk. He'd already planted the seed. She knew exactly what he wanted. Now he had to let his actions speak louder than his words. Not a problem at all. In his line of work, actions always got the job done.

"Why don't you go out on the deck and relax?" he suggested, rubbing his hand up and down her back. "I'll bring you some tea. I'm sure you packed an assortment."

Jenna wasn't a drinker, not of alcohol, anyway. Her mother had once battled alcoholism, but had been clean for the past several years. So, while booze was off the table for Jenna, Mac knew the girl never went out of town without her tea collection. It was one thing she took quite seriously. No doubt she'd brought the antique tin that he'd gotten her for Christmas several years back. She'd seen the piece before an auction and had coveted the item, so Mac had anonymously placed the bids and gotten it for her as a surprise.

Nearly all bidding was anonymous.... But in this instance, he'd simply done something for his best friend, not for a billionaire client or the good of the family business.

Jenna pulled away and offered him a tired smile. "You're too good to me."

"I'll let you return the favor one day when I need you to pretend to be my fiancée," he joked. "Do you want a particular flavor?"

He watched the sway of her hips as she walked away. "Surprise me."

Mac laughed. She'd better watch what she asked for. Because by the end of this week, she'd be surprised all right. Seduction would never taste sweeter.

This might be the only chance to be this close to her, at her invitation. He planned to take full advantage of this week posing as her boyfriend. This was the exact opportunity he needed to get closer, by her invitation. He planned on playing his role flawlessly every minute of the next seven days.

* * *

Jenna crossed her ankles and stared out at the sparkling water just beyond her deck. With bright blue skies, the sun just on the horizon and her best friend brewing her tea, Jenna should be the most relaxed woman in the world.

Unfortunately, she couldn't relax when her lips were still tingling, her body was still aching and her mind was still reeling from her best friend's bombshell admission that he wanted to sleep with her.

She hadn't seen that coming. Yes, he'd tried to pick her up with some overly cheesy line many years ago, but Mac was a professional flirt. And they'd agreed not to take things in that direction back then. She'd told him she only wanted long term and she knew he couldn't offer permanence. No way would she make herself vulnerable when she knew nothing serious could come of her attraction to Mac.

But the way he'd kissed her, held her and stared into her eyes when he delivered that shocking blow…this man wasn't joking anymore. He was full-on trying to get her into his bed, and if she wasn't careful that's exactly where she'd find herself. Talk about an awkward morning after, and she just couldn't risk their friendship.

Stretching her arms out, she clasped her fingers behind her head. She really needn't get too worked up, though. Mac loved women and women, understandably, loved Mac. He had charm, power, a killer body and a smile that could melt the clothes right off your body.

But she had to remind herself the proposition had nothing to do with her personally. Mac was a world-renowned playboy. He'd earned his reputation by his actions over the years and Jenna wasn't naive. She'd seen firsthand what a damaging relationship could do. Granted, her parent's situation was much different, but her mother had still been crushed, destroyed and ultimately had turned to the bottle when Jenna's father walked out. Jenna didn't think she'd ever be dependent on alcohol, but she was vulnerable to the same emotional damage her mother had suffered. Jenna knew if she allowed herself to be intimate with Mac two things would happen: she would love every single erotic moment, and he'd leave her wanting more as he walked away. She refused to be dependent on her feelings, to let her emotions lead her common sense around on a leash. Jenna had to keep a level head about this and remember everything going on here was all for show.

So, while her lips may still be tingling from their earlier encounter, she had to ignore the urge to take what he so eagerly offered.

Mac's heavy footsteps hit the wood deck. "Here you go."

After handing her a glass of iced tea, peach she guessed from the scent, he walked to the edge of the deck and took a seat. With the huts and decks built right on the water, his feet rested in the crystal-clear ocean. His black T-shirt pulled across his broad shoulders. His dark, unruly hair curled just slightly on the ends. Jenna didn't care that she was checking out her best friend. She'd done it for years, and the older he got, the sexier Mac O'Shea became. This combination ocean/hottie view was definitely one she would be enjoying all week.

"So, tell me what's on the agenda for tomorrow." He threw a glance over his shoulder, offering her an evil, lopsided grin. "Kissing on the beach, you unable to keep your hands off me, frolicking in the ocean?"

Jenna took a hearty drink of her iced tea and rolled her eyes. "I think we'll stick with hand holding, a few hugs and some lingering glances. Can you handle that?"

With a shrug, he turned back to the ocean. "I can handle anything. I'm in Bora Bora with my best friend and I have everything under control with the upcoming auction. I could use a few days to rest up, even if I'm pretending to be in love."

A sliver of guilt started to course through her. "I know I'm putting you in a weird position, so if you want to back out, do it now before we get too far."

Mac turned, rested his back against one of the posts and drew one knee up as he met her gaze. "Jenna, I came here for you. If you need me to hold your hand, literally, to get through this next week, that's what I'm going to do. Stop worrying about my feelings or whatever else is going through that head of yours."

She sat up in her lounge chair and swiveled her legs to the side. Clutching her glass, she watched the drops of condensation slide down it, disappearing beneath the pads of her fingers. Worry gnawed at her and she knew she could be totally honest with Mac about her deepest concern.

"I don't want things to get awkward between us."

"Then stop analyzing it to death," he commanded. "We'll be fine. The ex will think you've moved on, your sister's wedding will be over and done, and you'll be back in Miami by next week."

In theory everything sounded so perfect and easy. Reality always had other plans, though.

Jenna took another drink before looking over to Mac, who was still staring at her. "Do you want something to eat? The resort actually stocked our kitchen. I don't even want to know what Amy paid for all of this."

Mac shook his head. "Nah. I was joking earlier. I'm too tired to eat, anyway. That whirlwind trip to Barcelona wiped me out."

"I'm sure the lovely Lolita you left behind with a smile would take that as a compliment."

Mac pulled his other foot from the water and hopped to his feet. "Lolita was nowhere to be found," he retorted as he took a seat beside her on the lounge chair. "The trip was all business. I didn't see one naked woman the entire time."

Gasping, Jenna mocked him. "No wonder you're so cranky. And here I'm putting a damper on your social life because you have to pretend to be taken."

"We don't have to pretend," he replied with raised brows. "Say the word and we'll make use of this lounge chair."

Jenna sprang to her feet and headed toward the open doorway. "Chill out, stud. I have enough to handle without feeding your overactive hormones."

Mac followed her into the hut. Jenna rinsed her empty glass and just as she went to set it on the counter, it slipped from her hands and shattered all over the ceramic tile.

Cursing beneath her breath, she glanced down, trying to figure out how to get out of the mess without cutting her bare feet.

"Don't move."

Mac stepped carefully around the shards and seconds later lifted her into his arms.

"Put me down. I'm heavy."

Halting his steps, Mac met her gaze, his face mere inches above hers. "You're not heavy, Jenna. You're perfect. I won't want to hear that from your mouth again."

Closing her eyes, praying for the humiliation to pass, Jenna sighed. "Just put me down. I'll put some shoes on and get this mess cleaned up."

"I can get it."

"You're going to cut yourself," she argued, though the point was moot now.

"Better me than you."

He placed her on the sofa and stood back, his hands on his hips, his narrowed eyes daring her to argue. Jenna held her hands up in defeat. She wasn't fighting with him. She chose her battles wisely. Besides, she had to admit she rather liked this whole knight-to-her-rescue thing.

Moments later, once the glass was all discarded and he'd swept the floor thoroughly, Mac returned and sat on the table in front of the sofa. Straddling her legs, he reached down and placed one of her feet on his leg. When he started to examine her, she pulled her foot away.

"I'm fine. I wasn't cut."

"You're sure?"

Jenna snorted. "I think I'd know, Mac. Calm down. Were you cut?"

He merely shrugged. The man was infuriating at times.

"You know, you could've called someone to come clean that up."

Shaking his head, he replied, "By the time someone came, I would've been done. It's not a big deal."

Mac O'Shea might have been a billionaire, he might have been a mysterious, powerful man, but he wasn't lazy. He worked hard and always remembered that just because someone had money didn't make them better than anyone else. His father had instilled that value in all of the kids, and Jenna admired Mac and his siblings for being so conscious of other people's feelings...unless those people crossed the line. Then the O'Sheas left no room for negotiation, if the rumors were correct. Still, overall they were good people. She knew about the charities they silently donated to. She'd overheard Mac talking on the phone once to Laney, his sister, but Jenna hadn't said a word. She was proud the family didn't boast about the fact they shared their wealth. That's what giving was all about.

The sun had sunk lower, sending a soft glow into the hut through the wide opening leading to the deck. Fatigue was starting to take over and she was running out of steam. She needed to rest up if she was going to pull off this charade for the next seven days. Who knew when Martin would arrive, and she wanted to be ready.

"I'll sleep here on the sofa," she told Mac. "Actually, I'm so tired, I think I could pass out on that hammock out on the deck."

Mac simply shook his head. "You're sleeping in the bed and so am I. We're adults, Jenna. We've been friends for years."

Yeah, well, she'd never lain next to her best friend and attempted to sleep after he kissed her as if he needed her more than air. How could she sleep if his hard body brushed against hers in the middle of the night? What if she rolled over and her parts touched his parts? Because then a new level of awkward would settle in and that was the last thing she wanted.

"Whatever you're worried about, stop." His demand was loud and clear. "Go to bed. I'll be in later."

Yeah, that's precisely what she worried about.

Three

"We may have found something."

Mac sat up straighter and glanced toward the closed bedroom door where Jenna had disappeared over an hour ago.

"The scrolls?" he asked his associate Ryker in a hushed tone. But Ryker was so much more than an associate. He was a brother, a friend, an enforcer. He might not share the same blood, but he was practically family.

And he'd found information on the infamous scrolls. The nine pieces of family heritage they'd been chasing for decades. Their ancestor was an Irish monk who'd been chosen to transcribe Shakespeare's early works. The scrolls were invaluable…and still missing. They'd been in the O'Shea family up until they'd lost everything in the Great Depression, then they'd vanished.

Under the direction of their father, they'd followed countless leads. Once Patrick had passed and Braden had taken control, he'd gone to the point of origin at an old estate in Boston that used to be owned by the O'Sheas. The scrolls were last known to be there, yet his family was still on a damn wild goose chase. Granted, had he not gone to the starting point, Braden never would've met Zara, the love of his life. Zara now owned the home which used to be in their family. Even she had searched her home, but nothing had turned up.

Mac, his brother Braden and their sister Laney were ready to fulfill their late father's request and find these missing heirlooms, but so far they'd had no luck. Ryker, the go-to guy who was more like a brother than an employee, had proved himself to be relentless in finding the scrolls, in fulfilling a dying man's wish—no matter where in the world he had to follow the trail.

"I'm actually boarding the jet now," Ryker stated. "I'll be heading to Chicago on a tip from McCormick's."

McCormick's. If the O'Sheas worried about rivals, McCormick's would be top of the list. But, Mac's family had been in the industry much longer and had far longer reaches into that world…both political and civilian. That, coupled with everything they had going on behind the scenes, definitely made them the most sought-out auction house in the world. They could get the job done, fly under the legal radar and have transactions completed quickly and efficiently. Their clients never knew the details of how things were handled, they only knew O'Shea's was discreet and got things done.

"Is this tip from a reliable source?" Mac asked.

"Reliable enough," Ryker said. "I'll keep you posted, but Braden was busy at some event with Zara and they couldn't be bothered, so I had to act fast. Where are you, anyway? Still in Barcelona?"

Mac came to his feet and glanced out the open doorway toward the inky water, shimmering only slightly from the moon peeking from behind the clouds. Bora Bora was one of the most beautiful places on the planet… it was also one of the most romantic. Not that he did the whole candlelight-on-the-beach kind of thing. He was more of a slam the bedroom door with his foot as he plastered a willing woman against the wall and claimed her type of guy.

"I'm in Bora Bora with Jenna. She had a family emergency." Sort of. "I'll be home in a week, but let me know as soon as you discover anything, no matter how minor."

"Will do."

Mac disconnected the call and gripped his cell in his hand. Every time there was another lead, he got anxious. After years of letdowns, Mac knew he shouldn't get his hopes up, but all of this searching had to pay off at some point, didn't it? Because none of them would stop until these scrolls were found. Unfortunately, Patrick O'Shea had passed before he could fulfill that vow. The heart attack that claimed his father was sudden. He'd gone in for surgery, knowing there was a risk, but it was his only option for survival. They'd lost him on the table.

Mac didn't know if he'd ever get used to the idea of his father not being around. Then again, he didn't want to get used to the loss. He wanted to remember his father for the powerful, loving family man he was. He may have been a hard-ass outside his inner circle, he may have had more blood on his hands than a corrupt politician, but Patrick O'Shea was loyal to those close to him. Mac missed that man every minute of every day and would continue to honor his father's legacy and work with his siblings to make the O'Shea name as reputable as ever.

With his mind spinning in so many directions, Mac was too wound up to go to bed. Well, he was too wound up to sleep. Getting between the sheets with Jenna right now wouldn't be wise. He wanted her so damn bad, with a fierceness he'd not allowed himself to feel before. She wasn't ready, though.

His priority for the next few days was to make Jenna smile, to make her life worry-free and to get her to see just how easy it would be to be intimate and still be friends. He wasn't looking for a lifetime commitment; they were already best friends and that was about as close to someone as he was willing to get.

Given the family business, he was used to keeping certain things close to his chest. He didn't want to get too involved with anyone because he doubted there was a woman in the world who would put up with his lies. And he would lie to Jenna—he *had* lied to her. He had no choice with his lifestyle, and he wasn't about to apologize for it.

He'd been born an O'Shea, born into a world that was glamorous, powerful and, more often than not, deceitful. He was proud of his name, dirty rumors be damned. Because, overall, the name O'Shea brought prestige and power. No one questioned them to their faces. And Mac would stop at nothing to help fulfill his father's dying wish in getting back the scrolls. At all costs. They'd been missing long enough and he wanted to be the one to bring them back to their rightful place.

Turning back around, Mac eyed the bedroom door once again. Was she asleep? Was she tossing and turning? Was she fantasizing about the offer he'd given? One way to find out. Stripping off his shirt, Mac tossed it to the sofa and padded toward the bedroom. No matter what she was doing, Mac was going in. He wasn't tired, but there was no sense in delaying the inevitable. A smile spread across his face as he unbuttoned his shorts, slid the zipper down and let them fall to the floor. He stepped out of them and slowly turned the knob.

Wearing only his black boxer briefs, Mac entered the darkened room, took in the curvy shape beneath the sheet and headed to the other side of the bed. After flipping his phone to silent, he placed it on the bedside table and sank onto the edge of the bed.

Behind him the sheets rustled and Mac had a hard time not letting his imagination run away with him. He'd never had a sleepover with Jenna before. Oh, she'd fallen asleep during a movie several times when he visited her or she came to his place. But Mac had never spent the night with her and she certainly hadn't been planning on him sleeping in her room, so had she packed adequate pajamas? Did she sleep in the nude? All those lush curves, begging to be touched...

Mac eased back onto his pillow, crossed his ankles, laced his hands over his bare abdomen and stared up at the ceiling. The blades of the fan whirled in a slow, steady circle, giving off just enough of a light breeze to make the sheer curtains billow in front of the open window. The perfect setting for relaxation. For seduction. If this were any other woman, Mac wouldn't put forth so much effort, but he knew full well that being with Jenna would be worth the wait and definitely worth the exercise in self-control.

A soft moan filled the silence of the room as Jenna shifted beneath the sheet again. Apparently she had fallen asleep, but she was restless. Good. Selfishly, he wanted her to be on edge, to be aching because he sure as hell was lying here in a state of...well, he couldn't quite put the proper term to it.

Another moan escaped Jenna, this one louder, longer. Mac clenched his fists at his side. She was dreaming. His ego liked to think she was dreaming of him, of his proposition. The thought of her with another man irritated him, but he had no permanent claim on Jenna. Wanting intimacy with someone was completely different than wanting a happily-ever-after.

His eyes adjusted even more to the darkened room as he rolled over to watch her. A sheen of sweat covered her face; her lips were parted just enough to be even sexier than usual. The sheet slid down as she shifted again. What the hell was she wearing? Was that…yeah, she was wearing some type of maxi dress. Why?

Mac eased the sheet the rest of the way down her body. No wonder she was sweating. As soon as that layer was off, he stood and reached for the fan control, to kick it up on high. When he turned back to the bed, that long dress had ridden up on Jenna's thighs. Mercy, the woman was killing him.

He knew she was insecure about her body. They'd never talked about it because he wouldn't give that negativity any attention. To him, Jenna was absolutely perfect. He didn't want her to believe her shape defined her. There had to be some way to make her see herself the way he did. To realize that she was a voluptuous, stunning siren and she was valuable to anyone who took the time to appreciate her.

Jenna rolled to her side, facing him. Mac watched the swell of her breast threaten to move over the boundary of the scoop neck of the dress. A tan line ran up around her neck—he resisted the urge to run his finger along the pale skin.

That damn kiss had completely messed with his mind. While he'd always found her sexy as hell, now that he'd fully tasted her, he could think of nothing but tasting her again. For years he'd thrown out one sexual innuendo after another, but he wasn't kidding any longer. That kiss had changed something in him and as soon as he knocked her guard down and made her his, he could eradicate her from his system and they could circle back to this friendship thing.

Before he could roll away, her lids fluttered open, her eyes locking on to his. She blinked as she licked her lips, her hand moving up to adjust the top of her dress.

"Why are you staring at me?" she asked, her voice husky.

"You were dreaming." He wasn't about to answer her question. "And moaning."

Her eyes widened, then closed briefly before she met his gaze once again. "Did I wake you up?"

Mac shifted on his side more, propping his elbow on the pillow, his head in his hand. "I just came in here. You're sweating and wearing a dress to bed. Care to tell me why?"

The second he mentioned the dress, she jerked and adjusted the material back down. "I didn't have proper pajamas for a bedmate and I certainly didn't plan on you being in my bedroom with me."

Mac swallowed and fisted the sheet in front of him. "What did you pack?"

"Doesn't matter."

Stubborn to a fault. No wonder they got along so well. The push-pull part of their relationship was half the fun.

"What were you dreaming about?" he asked.

When she hesitated, he knew. Good. He liked knowing he was in her thoughts when she wasn't fully in control.

"Nothing much," she replied, her eyes darting away.

"With moans like that? I'd say it was something pretty amazing."

Jenna rolled over the other way, threw her legs over the side and offered him her back. "Drop it, Mac."

Such emotion for someone who wasn't dreaming of anything major. He was getting to her, already she was thinking of them together. Seducing her would be a cinch. But he didn't want to just seduce her, he wanted her to come to him.

"Change your clothes." When she glanced over her shoulder, he added, "You're hot, you're uncomfortable and you need to rest. Whatever you brought to sleep in, I think I can handle it."

After a moment, she nodded. She went to the chest of drawers, got something out and disappeared into the bathroom. A sliver of light slid from beneath the door and Mac had to force himself not to march in there and take what they both wanted. He only had a week, but he'd give her another day to come to terms with the fact they would be sleeping together in every sense of the word. Lying beside her would be a new test in self-control, but this was his Jenna and she deserved to be treated with respect.

So he'd lie here and be the perfect gentleman…for now. This would be completely new territory for him, but he was willing to make the sacrifice for an epic end result.

When Jenna came back out, he couldn't tell what she'd put on until she passed by the open window and the soft moonlight flickered across her body. The image lasted only a second, but long enough that he was reevaluating this gentlemanly decision. She wore a silk chemise that hugged her every hollow and curve. The lace trim around the dip just above her backside teased him. What would she do if he ran his finger beneath that edge? If he slid one of those thin, silky straps off her shoulder and showed her how good he could make her feel? Would she prefer the real thing to her dreams?

As she slipped in beside him, Mac gritted his teeth and wished like hell he'd opted to sleep on the deck in the hammock. If he left now, though, she'd have the upper hand and he never gave up control that easily.

"Good night, Mac."

Facing the opposite direction, Jenna slid the sheet up and over her shoulders as if she wanted an extra layer of defense. A sheet and a piece of satin wouldn't keep him away, but the fact she was so special to him would. Tomorrow was another day and all of this playing around in pretend-lovers' bliss would get to her. He'd make damn sure of it.

Okay, she'd done it. She'd made it through one night sleeping next to Mac and she'd even put on the chemise she'd packed. She loved barely there lingerie, it always made her feel sexy. Unfortunately, she'd risked putting silk and lace on with only one man, years ago…and that plan had backfired. She refused to make that mistake again.

Fortunately it had been dark last night and Mac hadn't seen her. This morning she'd gotten out of bed before him and could sneak off to shower and throw on another sundress before he got up. She'd thought for sure he'd sleep on the pull-out couch when she'd asked him to meet her here. Never would she have thought he'd use this situation to get closer to her…she should've known better.

"Tell me we're going to have a huge lunch after this flower thing because I'm starving."

Jenna laughed and swatted Mac on the chest as they walked toward the lobby of the resort. She'd received a call that the flowers she'd custom ordered had arrived and were in the walk-in refrigerator in the kitchen. Jenna was so excited to see all the buds and blooms in various colors. Her sister had wanted a variety because she hadn't been able to narrow down her colors to just a few.

Being able to work with fresh flowers for a wedding was always a joy for Jenna, but to be doing it for her sister was even more thrilling.

Jenna passed through the open entryway to the lobby and glanced to Mac. "You're always hungry. How do you not weigh five hundred pounds?" Damn men and their flawless metabolism.

"If I'd had more than yogurt and fruit for breakfast I wouldn't be so hungry."

"You're hangry. It's okay. I get that way myself."

His brow lifted behind his dark shades. "Excuse me?"

"Hangry. When you're hungry and angry," she explained with a shrug as she reached the counter. "I forgive you and I promise to get you a nice meal when we're done here."

She patted his cheek with her free hand and directed her attention to the lady waiting to assist them. After they were escorted toward the kitchen, the woman directed them to the tubs of flowers that had been set outside the back doors for Jenna to sort through. The manager had made sure a workspace was set up for Jenna, and the employees were told to let her in and out as often as she needed while she crafted the various arrangements and bouquets.

The next hour flew by in a whirlwind of buds, greenery and tissue wrappings. Jenna meticulously sorted each bundle, leaving the lilacs off to the side. She'd be taking those back to her bungalow, along with a few other bundles, to start working on the smaller bouquets. Those would fit in the refrigerator in her own kitchen and that way she wouldn't be scrambling to do so much the day before the wedding.

Jenna glanced at Mac who was enthralled by something on his phone. With his dark eyes drawn in, the muscle ticking in his jaw and the death grip with which he held his phone, Jenna knew something was wrong.

She laid the flowers down and reached across to touch his forearm. "What's going on?"

Blinking, he looked up. "Just reading an email. I need to make a call."

Jenna removed her hand as he came to his feet and headed out toward the breathtaking garden area and gazebo, probably where the employees took their breaks. As she watched Mac's shoulders tighten and tense beneath his blue T-shirt, Jenna wondered what could be so pressing. He glanced to the sky and shook his head as if frustrated with the person on the other end of the line. Whatever it was, she had no doubt this call was work related.

Mac's work was definitely something she knew very little about. Oh, sure, everyone knew the O'Sheas of Boston—the family, with their auction houses around the globe, was infamous. Mac had actually just opened two more US-based locations in Atlanta and Miami—she may have asked him to open one in Miami so she could see him more often. She'd had no idea he would actually do it and move down there to oversee the office.

But as successful as his family was, Jenna still didn't know what all the secrets were about and Mac would never betray his family's trust. She'd never known a man to be so loyal.

Her father certainly hadn't been. Jenna knew people were responsible for their own actions, but she couldn't help but blame the man for running out and leaving her mother to turn to the bottle. Those years were pure hell, but with love and the unshakeable bond between a mother and her daughters, Jenna and Amy were able to turn their mother around.

Mac shoved his cell into his pocket and headed back her way.

"You okay?" she asked, bundling up the flower assortment she needed to take back to the bungalow.

"Just work." He caught a cluster of tissue-wrapped greenery that had started to slide off the table. "We hired a new manager at the main office in Boston. I just needed to get her into Miami to handle some issues concerning the upcoming auction."

Guilt slid through her. "If you need to go, it's fine, really."

Mac reached for her hand and squeezed. "I'm not going anywhere. This is nothing I can't fix with a couple of phone calls. Now, tell me where to take these so you can feed me that promised lunch."

Rolling her eyes, Jenna came to her feet and pointed to a pile of flowers. "Be careful with those or you'll get yogurt and fruit again."

He picked up the bundle and laughed. "Not many things scare me, but I know if I lose one petal you'll torture me."

Jenna carried her own stack and headed out. She informed the staff that they could put the rest away and she'd be back tomorrow to get more. With the flowers in hand, Jenna led Mac back toward their bungalow. The sun was already bright and it was still early. This would be a perfect day to lounge on her deck, fiddle with arrangements and continue working on her tan. Though she knew she wouldn't be more beautiful than the bride,

Jenna wanted to be at her best when she had to walk next to her cheating jerk ex.

As soon as she saw a familiar figure heading her way, Jenna froze. It was as though she'd conjured up the devil himself. She knew the moment was coming, but she was hoping her ex would avoid her for the sake of saving face. Apparently his ego had gotten the best of him.

"Martin's here," she muttered, clutching the stems of her bundles even tighter. "Let's turn around."

"Like hell."

Before she knew what was happening, Mac shifted his stash of flowers in the crook of one arm and wrapped his other arm around her. In the same instant, his lips crushed hers, forcing her to hold on to him with her free hand and enjoy the ride. Mac's mouth demanded more and she was all too willing to give it. This kiss, if something so powerful could have such a simple term, didn't feel like an act at all. This felt more like a stepping stone to something more private and intimate. And it certainly wasn't like the one from the other day. This kiss held…promise.

Jenna's entire body heated. Tingling started low in her belly and she had aches in places she'd never ached before. Mac's hold on her tightened and Jenna couldn't prevent the moan that slipped from her lips.

Martin cleared his throat and Mac pulled away. His lopsided grin and a naughty gleam in his eye told Jenna he was enjoying this. Just another reason she couldn't let her heart tumble into this charade. Mac was a professional player. This game was well within his comfort zone. That made one of them.

Once Mac stepped to her side, his free arm still draped around her shoulders, Jenna got a good look at her ex… and he was fuming.

"What the hell are you doing?" he demanded, staring at Jenna. "I told you I'd be here so we could talk and you're with this guy? He's more of a liar and a cheater than I ever thought of being."

Before she could respond, Mac spoke up. "Apologize to her now."

Martin's narrowed gaze darted to Mac. "Who the hell are you to tell me anything? Jenna belongs with me."

Mac pulled his arm away and stepped between her and Martin. "Not anymore. I'm her fiancé."

Four

"I cannot believe you just did that."

Mac watched as Jenna stormed through their bungalow. She'd carefully set the flowers on the kitchen island and then took off pacing, throwing her arms in the air and muttering words that would make his Irish mother, God rest her soul, blush.

"I only wanted you to pretend to be my boyfriend," she yelled as she turned to pace in the other direction. "Then you go and tell me you want to be my lover, you have my mother and sister thinking we're quite serious and you tell my ex we're engaged."

Finally, she turned to face him, her hands propped on her hips, her chest heaving. "Are you going to say anything?"

Mac shrugged and placed his flowers next to hers. "That guy is an ass. I'm not sorry for what I said."

"Are you sorry for the position you put me in?"

Maybe a little, but Mac hadn't liked this ex. He'd had *possessive* written all over him and nobody laid a claim on Jenna. Well, this week Mac did, but there was no way in hell Mac would let a guy like Martin have another chance with Jenna. Mac knew the type Martin was—a wealthy playboy who got whatever he wanted…damn it. Mac had just described himself.

But still, Mac worked hard for everything he had and he'd work just as hard to make sure Jenna never had to deal with that jerk again. The fact that Martin knew of the O'Sheas was helpful. Mac didn't purposely hide behind his name, but clearly Jenna had spoken of him and that only made Mac feel even more protective of her.

"You called me here to help." Slowly he closed the space between them and rested his hands on her shoulders, bending his knees so he could look her in the eyes. "The whole *engaged* thing slipped out, but now that it has, we'll deal with it the same way as before. Once this week is over, we just explain to your family that we decided we're better off as friends."

Jenna let out a heavy sigh. "You make this sound so easy."

He stared down into her mesmerizing eyes. She had a way of drawing him in before he even knew what was happening. Jenna was one of the most important people in his life and he wouldn't let her down.

"Trust me?" he asked, tipping his head to hold her gaze.

Her features softened as her shoulders relaxed beneath his touch. "You know I do. And it's not just my family I'm worried about. I've dragged you into this—"

"Do I look like I mind?" he asked, offering her a smile.

"You look like you're having the time of your life."

She laughed. "Don't get so caught up that you forget we're just acting."

Oh, no worries there. No matter how amazing Jenna was, he didn't want to be tied down to anyone for a lifetime commitment. And that was exactly how he viewed marriage.

"I think I can handle kissing you in public and still remember that we're just friends," he told her.

Something flashed across her face, but before he could analyze what it was, the emotion was gone. He wanted inside that head of hers, wanted to know what she truly thought about this entire arrangement...about him. But perhaps it was better to be in the dark. Maybe the truth would have him running in the other direction. Emotions were one area he tried not to venture into.

"Now, what are we doing for lunch?" he asked.

Jenna grunted as she laid her hands flat on his chest and gave him a shove. "You have a one-track mind."

He raked his eyes over her body, then threw her a wink and a grin. "I actually have a couple tracks, but I'm a whiz at multitasking."

"Let me put these flowers in the fridge and then we can go get a bite." She maneuvered around Mac and grabbed the flowers, carefully placing them on the shelf she'd emptied just for this reason. "While we're out we need to be holding hands. Maybe you can brush my hair back from my shoulders and look at me when I pretend not to notice. You know, do whatever people in love are supposed to do."

Silently, he closed the gap between them and came within a breath of her. She jumped at his nearness. "And what will you be doing?"

The cool air from the refrigerator did nothing to control the heat inside her. As she straightened and turned, he was literally right there.

"Um…" What was the question? Oh, right. "I guess I'll be smiling and nodding and hanging on your every word."

Mac brushed her hair over her shoulders, his fingertips trailing over her bare skin there, then up her neck to her jaw as he framed her face. "No, you're not that type of woman, Jenna."

Why was he looking at her like that? Did he give off that "I want to devour you" vibe to his other lovers?

"I'm not?" she whispered.

His thumb brushed along her bottom lip. "No. You're in control. You don't even realize it, but any man worth having you would fall under your spell. He'd hang on your every word and you would hold the power."

Jenna's breath caught in her throat. She held power? Over whom? Because she might not be experienced in relationships, but she knew she'd never held control over anyone.

"When we go out, I will be the one spellbound. We'll show this ex exactly what he threw away, because you are worth hanging on to."

Right. The ex. That's what all of this was about… right? Why was she having such a difficult time focusing? Oh, yeah. Because Mac had her backed up against an appliance. His body was practically molded against hers and he was looking at her as if she was the main course and dessert all wrapped up in one delectable package.

Jenna couldn't afford to get tangled up in her emotions. Mac wasn't good for her; they wanted two very different things in life. But now they were each playing a role and she had to remember it was only for a few more days. Getting swept away by the act of being Mac

O'Shea's lover was only asking for heartache…no matter how much her heart clenched when he looked at her with desire in his eyes.

Reaching up to grip his wrists, Jenna eased his hands away from her face. "There's a great restaurant here at the resort and normally you need a reservation, but our wedding party has been given full run of the place. They have some amazing local dishes. Let me change and we'll head out."

As she stepped aside, the fridge door shut. Just as soon as she moved, Mac blocked her path.

"Am I making you nervous, Jenna?"

Nervous? No. Achy, needy and ready to rip his clothes off? Yes.

"Not at all," she replied with a wide smile. "I'm worried about pulling this off, especially considering how angry Martin was earlier. He doesn't like to be told no."

"Yeah, well, I don't like the way he talked to you." Mac looked as if he wanted to say more, but he finally stepped aside and motioned toward the bedroom. "Go get ready. I'll wait on the deck."

Jenna rushed to the bedroom and closed the door at her back. They were on the second day of this charade and she only prayed she could make it the final five. Surely this would get easier…it had to, for the sake of her sanity and her heart.

Lunch was amazing and there were no additional run-ins with Martin the Jerk. Mac hadn't met the man before today, but just one look was enough to know he wasn't good enough for Jenna. Mac was actually looking forward to another encounter with him. He'd prefer the next one to be away from Jenna, but whenever the opportunity presented itself, Mac would be prepared. Martin seemed too full of himself to just let Jenna go and be happy. Mac would see to it that Martin would never be able to hurt her again.

"You're scowling," she muttered as she looped her arm through his. "People are going to think we're fighting."

He patted her hand as he led her down the narrow path toward the beach. "Then we'll have to kiss and make up in public. I'm fine with that."

"You just like to kiss."

Shrugging, he threw her a glance. "You have a great set of lips. Who wouldn't like to kiss them?"

Jenna reached out to push aside a tropical plant hanging over the walkway. "We're pretending, no need to start laying on the charm."

"I wouldn't lie about something like that," he replied. As they hit the edge of the sand, he turned to her. "You do believe me, right? I may have to keep secrets from you to protect you and my family but when it comes to other things between us, you'll only get the full truth from me."

Jenna stared at him as if he were crazy. "Yeah, sure."

Before he could stop himself, he snaked his arms around her and pulled her flush against his body. He captured her squeal when he covered her mouth with his.

Mac gripped the back of her dress, fighting the urge to lift it up and whisk it over her head. They were in public, but she was seriously doing a number on his emotions. Mac had originally set out to seduce her, but now he also wanted to dismantle any insecurities she had, so when she moved on to the next guy, she would know her self-worth.

Damn. The next guy. Mac didn't think any guy would be good enough for Jenna.

When she moaned, Mac lifted his head slightly, nipping at her lips a few more times before pulling back.

He'd always been able stay detached from any woman, but Jenna was becoming his drug of choice and he saw no way to break the addiction until he got her into his bed.

"Did you see someone?" she asked, her lids fluttering open.

"I thought I saw your mom down the way." Okay, so that was a lie and he'd just told her he wouldn't lie to her, but he wasn't sorry—he was selfish. Pretending to squint and look in the distance, Mac shrugged. "My mistake."

Lacing his fingers through hers, Mac guided her down the beach. Jenna leaned against his side and he wondered if she was as turned on as he was from that kiss. Each time he tasted her he wanted more, he wanted to take it to another level. Did she even have those thoughts? She couldn't moan like that, couldn't lean so perfectly against his body and not want more. His ego swelled, but more than that, hope filled him because now he knew she would reciprocate his need, this ache that kept bouncing between them.

"My sister asked if you and I were free to have dinner with her and Nathan."

Water lapping at their bare feet, they strolled down the shoreline. Mac decided he really didn't want to share his Jenna time with anyone else. This week was about seducing his best friend, finally getting her where he'd wanted her since propositioning her years ago at a party. She'd never let herself respond to him before.

"When did they want to get together?" he asked, stroking the delicate area between her thumb and index finger.

"Well, the only free night is tonight. We have a dinner tomorrow, a party the following night, Friday is the rehearsal and Saturday is the wedding."

Damn. He'd been warned of all the "outings" this week, but he didn't realize his time would be so monop-

olized by wedding events. On the other hand, he could
totally play this to his advantage. If they were in public he
would have to be in lover mode. Maybe there were some
perks to these evening activities, after all. After making
Jenna moan, who knew what else he could pull out of her
during their remaining time on the island?

"I'll do whatever you want," he told her.

A mother and a father were splashing around at the
edge of the water with their toddler son. Mac didn't miss
the way Jenna stared at the family, the way her breath
caught before a soft smile spread across her face. He'd
bet she hadn't even noticed that she'd squeezed his hand
a bit tighter. Mac knew this is what she wanted, a family, children. Everything he couldn't offer, yet everything
she deserved. One of the many reasons this arrangement
had to be a temporary thing only. After she was out of
his system, he'd have to step aside and allow another man
to come into her life.

Best friends. That was the highest relationship status he had to give. Jenna would meet the right man and
start the family she wanted. The thought conjured up
a whole host of images Mac didn't appreciate. No man
would ever measure up, but that wasn't his decision to
make. Shame, that.

Still, when she found a man and things started getting serious, Mac would do a complete background check
and make sure the guy was squeaky clean because Jenna
deserved a man on the right side of the law, a man with
no secrets.

A man totally the opposite of Mac.

Not that Mac wanted that settled-down family lifestyle. The whole marriage thing was working for Braden
and Zara, but Mac was just fine focusing on work, par-
tying when he could and hooking up with women who

were on the same playing field as he was. Life was good, so why mess it up?

Mac tugged on Jenna's hand to keep her moving. "Maybe going out tonight would be the best option," he told her. "That way Nathan can see us together as well and pass along to his best man that you're officially off the market and not interested in a reunion."

Jenna shoved her sunglasses up onto her head, pushing her dark strands back from her face. "Good idea. I'll let Amy know. You're too good to me, Mac."

With a laugh, he shook his head. "Nah. Remember, if you mess this act up, I get to cash in a favor at any time."

Jenna playfully nudged his side with her elbow. "I'm pulling this whole thing off beautifully so far, which means I'll get another favor. Don't get so cocky."

Up ahead, Mac caught sight of Martin talking with Nathan. Perfect opportunity to work this lover's angle and shove it right into Martin's face. Mac didn't just want to convince the guy that Jenna had moved on, Mac wanted to torture the man with what he'd let go.

"You ready to put those acting skills to the test again?" he asked, nodding straight ahead.

Her gaze followed his and she drew in a deep breath. "I'd rather just avoid him."

"You're not a coward."

Before she could protest further, he trudged forward. He told her a joke to get her laughing. Mission accomplished. Jenna's rich laughter had Martin's head whipping around in no time.

Game on, you sorry bastard.

Nathan waved with a smile, but his eyes were darting between Martin, Jenna and Mac. Mac figured he'd have to break the tension since he was the one who was adamant about this little meeting.

"Hey, Nathan." Mac greeted the man as if he'd known him forever. In actuality, he'd met him once when he and Amy had come to visit Jenna in Miami. "Jenna just told me we'll be going out tonight. Looking forward to it."

"Amy wasn't sure when you guys were free," Nathan replied. "I'll be sure to let her know. I hear congratulations are in order for the two of you, as well?"

Mac wrapped his arm around Jenna, pulling her closer to his side, ignoring the kick of just how comfortable he was playing the role of doting fiancé.

"Thanks. We didn't want to make a big deal of anything, since this is your week and I actually just surprised Jenna."

"Where's the ring?" Martin asked, his tone mocking, his gaze narrowed.

Without missing a beat, Jenna replied, "Mac is flying me to his favorite jeweler in Italy after the ceremony Saturday so I can choose the one I want."

Mac mentally high-fived her quick, clever response. She'd stiffened slightly against him, but she'd managed to squelch her nerves and fire back. Martin's expression was priceless and his silence was another win for Mac. Maybe Jenna could handle this role-playing just fine. His hand slipped to the curve of her hip. When he squeezed her there, she jumped slightly and attempted to shift. Mac held her right where he wanted her. Damn, those curves beneath his hand sent his mind into overdrive.

"If you'll excuse us, we were on our way back to our room. Haven't had enough alone time with my girl." Mac returned Martin's glare with a mocking wink before nodding to Nathan. "See you tonight."

Completely dismissing Martin, Mac guided Jenna back along a path that would take them toward the bungalows nestled on the water.

"Nice job," he muttered when they were far enough away. "I actually do have a jeweler in Italy."

"Where I'm sure your female entourage is well supplied," she tossed back.

Was that a hint of…jealousy? Interesting. Definitely useful information.

"It's okay, babe. I'll make it up to you. Do you prefer diamonds or emeralds? My jeweler made this gorgeous diamond necklace for me once. Personally, I think rubies because you get fired up sometimes and—"

Jenna jerked from his grasp. "This isn't real so don't lump me with your collection of arm candy."

Mac didn't even get to defend himself before she stomped off toward the bungalow. He followed her because if they were having a lover's spat in public, he sure as hell planned on making up in private.

But what the hell had gotten into her? He'd swear she was jealous, but she'd pointed out on numerous occasions that this situation was false. So why the narrowed gaze? Why the hurt lacing her tone?

Mac caught up to her just before she could slam the door. He was about to find out.

Five

This entire situation was getting out of hand and they were only on day two. Why had she thought this would ever work? For a split second, which was more than she could afford, she'd let her emotions take control, shoving aside common sense. When Mac had palmed her side, sliding his hand over her, she'd become fully engulfed in this charade. A charade she'd started.

Plus, her emotions were not getting the message to stay detached. When Mac had mentioned he actually had a jeweler, Jenna knew without a doubt he'd taken women there. Jealousy, table for one.

Gritting her teeth, Jenna tried to regain some control over her self-induced rage. This whole situation was her fault. Any hurt, anger or envy she had spearing through her was all brought on by her need to rid herself of Martin.

The door to the bungalow slammed behind her, but

Jenna kept her back turned. She'd let her control slip. In all the years she and Mac had been friends, she'd joked about his other women, but she'd never, ever shown him how much she hated his playboy lifestyle. The moment had literally swept her away.

Jenna actually hated the jet-setting, womanizing part of his life even more than the secrets surrounding the mafia rumors. She had to say no to him because of his excessive lifestyle. She wanted to be special to any man she was involved with and being with Mac in an exclusive way wasn't an option. He'd never made it a secret that he loved women, that he never wanted to settle down and find "the one."

"Jenna."

She stiffened at his demanding tone. Starting this second, she was back in control. This was her life and she needed to remember that Mac was her best friend. Always loyal, always willing to do anything for her…taking things any further would be a mistake. He'd come down here to help without hesitation and she wouldn't repay him by dragging him into the middle of this battle between her heart and her mind.

Jenna spun around and met his questioning gaze. "Sorry. I didn't mean to go all possessive girlfriend on you out there. I got caught up in the moment."

Shaking his head, Mac crossed his arms over his broad chest. "You don't like the idea of me buying jewelry for other women."

No point in lying. "Fine. I don't."

With a defiant tilt of her chin, Jenna adjusted her sundress and mimicked his stance as she crossed her arms. "You flaunt women all the time and doing it now is inappropriate."

There. That sounded convincing, didn't it? Those penetrating eyes of his raked over her, sending shivers racing through her body. How could the man be so potent from across the room? Did he have a clue as to the damage he could do to her? Did he have any idea how difficult it had been for her to even ask him to step in?

Jenna was starting to wonder if she'd made a mistake. Too late for hindsight now.

"I had the necklace made for Laney on her twenty-first birthday." The simple explanation made her feel utterly foolish…as she should because she had zero hold over this man.

"You were jealous," he stated.

Jenna quirked a brow. "I was not. I expect you to remember what we're doing this week and what your role is."

Like a panther to its prey, Mac stalked across the room, his eyes locked onto hers. "Oh, I remember exactly what I'm doing here this week. The question is, do you?"

He stopped within a breath of her. His hands came up, tugging her arms loose until they fell to her sides, then he closed that final sliver of space. She had to tip her head up to look at him.

"Do I what?"

A muscle ticked in his jaw as he slid his hand up her arm, curled his fingers over her shoulder and replied, "Do you remember what our roles are? Seems to me you may have slipped into the position of my lover a bit too easily. Makes me wonder if you really do want to take advantage of this situation."

Unable to think of some witty, snappy comeback, Jenna skirted around him and headed to the fridge. Grabbing the flowers, she unwrapped the layers of tissue and laid everything out on the kitchen table.

"We're not lovers, Mac." Her hands were shaking, but

hopefully if she kept them busy, Mac wouldn't notice. "We're friends. Don't read into this."

In a flash, Mac reached out and gripped her hand. "This? Are you referring to your shaky hands or the fact you can't look me in the eye when you lie? Or maybe you wonder what it would be like if we did sleep together and you're afraid to admit it out loud."

Without looking up, she jerked her hand back and attempted to separate the bundle of lilacs. "I've wondered," she admitted. "Of course I have, but that doesn't mean I'm going to let it happen."

When he said nothing, when silence filled the air like an unwanted third party, Jenna dropped the flowers and rested her palms flat on the table. With a heavy sigh, she dropped her head between her shoulders.

"Mac, after this week I still want you to be my best friend. No matter what you say, no matter what you may think is a good idea now, if we slept together we couldn't take it back."

Mac cupped her chin and turned her head. Jenna forced her eyes on his, because appearing weak was not an option.

"When I sleep with you, I won't want to take it back."

Jenna gasped at all the veiled promises in that statement. A reply was impossible as Mac slid his mouth over hers, but not in a demanding way like last time. No, this kiss was slower, seductive, yet more commanding.

The power she'd thought she possessed where Mac was concerned vanished the second his lips silently demanded all of her attention.

When he pressed his palm flat against her back, Jenna fell against his solid, defined chest. Instinctively, her arms looped around his neck, her fingers threaded through his coarse hair. Mac lifted his mouth from hers for the briefest of moments before changing the angle and going back in for more.

More urgent now, he reached behind her. Tissue paper rustled and a second later he gripped her waist with his hands, lifting her to the edge of the table. On every level she knew this was a mistake. Mac was used to this, to taking what he wanted when he wanted it. Jenna was more of a thinker, a planner…a dreamer. She couldn't afford to be selfish and live directly in the moment. There would be consequences for every single action.

But right now, with his lips covering hers, then roaming along her jaw, Jenna tipped her head back and arched her body, consequences be damned.

"You taste so damn good," he muttered against her skin.

Jenna continued to clutch the back of his shirt, battling herself as to whether she should push him away or let this glorious moment continue. How could she ignore this inferno raging between them? She'd never felt so alive, so out of control and on the verge of something utterly blissful.

The pounding on her bungalow door brought every tantalizing thought to a halt. Mac's lips froze on the hollow part of her neck.

"Expecting company?" he asked, his voice husky.

Unable to speak, Jenna loosened her grip and shook her head.

Mac's intense, dark gaze raked over her body as he slowly pulled away. Jenna realized her legs were spread wide to accommodate his body, her dress hiked up high on her thighs. Jenna jerked the hem down and hopped off the table. Mac moved across the room just as more pounding shook the door.

When he yanked the door open with more force than

necessary, Jenna caught Martin's angry gaze. His eyes darted from Jenna to Mac and back to her. Well, this is what she wanted...wasn't it? She wanted him to see that she and Mac were serious. There couldn't be any doubt as to what they'd been doing...or about to do. Her hair was tousled all around her shoulders, most likely her face was flushed and Mac was breathing a bit harder than usual. Her body was still very much tingling from the encounter.

Oh, mercy, had she honestly been about to have sex with her best friend on the kitchen table? *Keep it classy, Jenna.*

"Sorry, this is a party for two," Mac said as he started to close the door.

Martin put his hand up, blocking the action. "Jenna. I need to speak with you. Alone."

"You won't be seeing my fiancée alone. Ever." Mac's voice had taken on a deadly, menacing tone, quite different from the sexy rasp he'd delivered only moments ago.

"Get the hell out of the way."

Jenna stepped forward, placed a hand on Mac's back and glared at Martin. "Whatever you want to say, do it quick."

Mac tensed beneath her palm, but since this wasn't a real relationship, she wasn't about to let him ride to her rescue this time. Jenna could handle her own problems.

"Give me another chance. I know we can work this out." Martin's eyes seemed to implore her. "You don't want to marry this guy. He'll ruin you."

Before she could stop him, Mac launched forward and fisted Martin's shirt. "Get the hell out of here."

Mac shoved him back out onto the deck leading to the bungalow. Jenna knew enough about Mac to know this was not the time to step in. He was angry, he was taking charge and he wouldn't want her to intervene, even if this situation was all about her.

Martin knocked Mac's hands away and took another step back. "You'd rather take a shot with this criminal than give me a second chance?" Martin asked. "That's not the Jenna I know."

Normally, Jenna wouldn't side with a guy who was so aggressive, but she knew Mac. This was for show. He was only going along with her request to make their relationship look authentic. Wasn't he?

He wasn't about to unleash his rage here. Surely not. Mac definitely had a temper, but since none of this was real, perhaps he'd keep himself in check.

"You need to go," she told Martin.

Once again his eyes darted between her and Mac before settling on her. "I hope you come around before it's too late. The rumors surrounding his family are enough—"

Mac punched Martin in the face, sending Martin's head flying back. Martin stumbled as he reached up to feel his jaw. Jenna gasped, gripping the door. Clearly Mac's restraint had snapped.

"He just proved my point," Martin spat out before turning and stomping away. "This isn't what you need, Jenna."

Despite the heat, a shiver rippled through her. Mac had gone too far, in more ways than one. Her body still trembled from having his mouth and hands all over her. Their relationship had crossed the friendship line because there was no way she could erase that memory. Then he'd gone and assaulted Martin. Granted, Martin was goading Mac on purpose, but Mac had lost his temper...an O'Shea family trait.

The polar opposite personas of Mac had been revealed

within a span of five minutes. How could he be two completely different people?

Unsure of what to say, Jenna remained silent and went back inside. Her eyes immediately landed on the table, on the cleared-off spot where Mac had set her. The man could make her totally forget all common sense. But seeing him become so angry had snapped her back to reality.

"Jenna—"

Keeping her back to the door, she held up her hand. "No. I don't want your apology."

"I wasn't going to give you one," Mac retorted. "I'm not sorry I hit him. Nobody insults my family and nobody disrespects you. That bastard did both."

Something about the way he was so adamant about defending those he loved made him even more attractive. But still, she had to wonder just how far he planned on taking this charade, not to mention how often his anger got the better of him. She'd heard things, ugly things, but she'd never seen Mac get violent before.

Jenna spun around. "I asked you to play the part of my boyfriend. Maybe I should've made things clearer from the start." Gathering up the flowers on the table, she carefully repackaged them, wondering when she would ever find a moment's peace to actually do her sister's wedding arrangements. "I didn't want a fake fiancé, I didn't want you to punch my ex and I didn't want you to cross the boundaries of our friendship by kissing me."

Mac remained still, eerily so, as he locked his eyes on hers. "The fiancé reference slipped out. I will apologize for saying that, but I'll never apologize for hitting a man who cheated on you and put you second in his life. I'm not sorry he'll be wearing my fist impression on his face."

Now he moved closer, closing the gap between them in two strides. "Don't look at me like that, Jenna. It's still me. I'd never raise my hand to a woman. I protect what's mine and no matter what's going on here, fake or real, you're mine."

Jenna's breath caught.

"And I sure as hell will not apologize for kissing you," he went on. "You didn't say no. Far from it. I've wanted to for years and I plan on doing it again. This week, Jenna, you belong to me as more than my friend. You started this and I'm finishing it."

He glanced down to the watch on his wrist. "Better shower up. We have a double date in an hour."

With that, he stalked out the back door to the hammock and relaxed as if he didn't have a care in the world, as if he was oblivious to the turmoil that raged within her. He'd delivered that emotionally packed speech, got her hormones good and jumbled then just turned to leave?

And she was his for the week? As in...*his*?

Both fear and excitement coursed through her. What type of beast had she unleashed?

Six

Mac pulled out the chair for Jenna. Once she was seated, he moved her hair from her shoulder and placed a kiss on her bare, sun-kissed skin. Her familiar floral scent mocked him. He knew firsthand that she dabbed her favorite perfume beneath her ears and put a dot between her breasts. Not only had he seen her do it a time or two, but when he'd been making a path from her neck to her chest, he'd inhaled that scent and he'd wanted more.

"This is so exciting." Amy beamed from the other side of the table. "I'm so happy for you guys and I'm really glad we could carve out this time to spend together. After all, we'll all be family soon enough."

Family? No. His family was his brother, sister, Ryker and Jenna. That was all. Small, simple, effective in making his life complete.

"I finished one of the small bouquets today," Jenna stated, as if she wanted this conversation to take another path, too. "It's even more beautiful than I thought it would be."

Yeah, instead of taking hours to get ready like most women he knew, Jenna had opted to work on an arrangement, then had showered and transformed into evening-ready in minutes. She was stunning tonight with her bare shoulders exposed. Her dress hugged those curves he was dying to get back beneath his hands.

Amy reached across the table and patted Jenna's arm. "I didn't ask you to do the flowers because you're my sister. I asked because you're the best."

Settling back in his seat, Mac could relax a bit more now that the sisters had fallen into their easy chatter. The waitress popped over to their table to take their drink orders. Mac and Nathan ordered the local beer on tap, while the ladies ordered a house wine and slid right back into all things wedding.

"Don't look so glum," Nathan stated with a laugh. "It's not that bad. And if she's happy, then that's all that matters."

Mac grunted. "I think eloping would be the easiest."

Amy gasped, focusing her attention on Mac. "You don't mean that. Jenna has always dreamed of a big wedding. She even has our mother's wedding gown in storage because she wants that vintage feel."

Apparently word traveled fast and Jenna had already discussed the "engagement" with her sister. Mac glanced at Jenna who was waving her hand in the air. "I'll be happy with any wedding, Amy. So long as it's to the man I love. I'll get my happily-ever-after," she assured her sister.

Jenna didn't meet Mac's stare. When he reached beneath the table to slide his hand over her leg, she shifted away just enough so that no one could see, but her silent message delivered a blow.

He'd hurt her earlier. He'd hurt her with his own self-ishness and lack of control. But when that bastard Martin had spouted off about Mac's family...well, he'd been looking for an excuse to punch the guy since he found out Martin had cheated on Jenna.

The waitress brought their drinks and took their orders. The open restaurant provided a view of the crystalline ocean, which glowed even more in the moonlight, palm trees swaying in the gentle breeze and couples strolling around hand in hand. The carefree lifestyle here would be so easy to get lost in; it was the perfect romantic setting, but he wasn't here for romance and his plan of seduction was backfiring in a major way.

Jenna deserved more than a fling. Mac took a hard pull from his beer and realized he was no better than Martin—as difficult as that was to admit. Martin had used her and Mac was attempting to do the same. Oh, Mac could justify his means by saying he'd always wanted her physically, which was true, but after this week he would go back to his life and Jenna would be left with...what? She didn't have feelings for him beyond friendship, but she was the type of woman who wanted that fairy-tale ending. Hadn't her sister just stated as much?

The only role Mac would ever play in a fairytale would be a villain. The villain never got the princess.

"Mac?"

Blinking, he sat his glass back down and looked to Amy. "I'm sorry, what?"

"I asked what happened." She nodded toward his injured hand still curled around his frosted mug.

"He had a slight altercation," Jenna chimed in. "No big deal."

Oh, hell, no. She wasn't coming to his defense or making lame excuses for him.

"I punched Martin."

Jenna sighed and dropped her head. Amy jerked back in her seat and Nathan narrowed his eyes.

"Why?" Amy demanded in a whispered tone.

"He cheated on Jenna and—"

"And nothing," Jenna stated, her voice rising over his. "Let's just leave this conversation for another time."

"He cheated on you?" Amy asked, her wide eyes turning to her sister. "I knew you guys broke up, but you never said why. Oh, honey, I'm so sorry you have to walk with him during the ceremony."

Mac clenched his teeth. The thought of Martin getting close to Jenna only made him see red all over again.

Amy turned to Nathan. "Did you know about this?" she demanded.

Nathan held his hands up in his defense. "He's my best friend, but I had no clue. I'd say he didn't tell me for obvious reasons."

Jenna reached for her wineglass. "Seriously, it happened a few weeks ago and I didn't want to ruin the wedding, so let's forget this conversation ever happened."

As she sipped her wine, she turned just enough to glare at Mac. He wasn't going to apologize. Amy and Nathan needed to know what kind of asshat was in their wedding party posing as a friend and all-round good guy.

Mac couldn't help but smile at the thought of the jerk sporting a shiner for the ceremony. Probably not something Amy would find amusing, but Mac sure did. They should be thankful Mac hadn't broken the guy's jaw, or worse.

"Please, don't let this ruin anything," Jenna begged.

Amy studied her sister and finally nodded. "So, tell

me what you've decided on for your wedding. Surely you have a date in mind or some details."

Hell. He was going to need something stronger than beer to get through this.

"Actually, this is all still so new to us."

Yeah, like two days.

"I want to focus on your wedding before thinking about my own," Jenna went on. "Did the resort get with you on the time I can start setting up in the dining area for the reception?"

"They told me after the rehearsal would be fine. Does that give you enough time?"

"Of course." Jenna's tight smile implied the arrangement was anything but fine, but she'd never tell her sister anything different.

Nathan asked Mac about the auction business and Mac kept his answers vague. Though O'Shea's was thriving even more than usual, Mac's mind was on the scrolls and how Ryker was doing with his lead. Ryker wasn't one to just send random check-ins, though. He wouldn't contact anyone until he discovered something substantial.

When Mac's cell vibrated in his pocket, he slipped it out just enough to see his sister's name on the screen.

"Excuse me," he stated as he came to his feet. "I need to take this."

His sister wasn't one to chat on the phone for fun, so the fact that she was calling had him on alert. Shoving his chair back, he offered a smile in reply to Jenna's worried look.

"Laney." He answered the phone as he walked from the table and out onto a fairly empty dock.

"Would you tell the family Neanderthal to stop checking on me?" his sister demanded.

Mac flinched at the anger lacing her voice. Laney

wasn't an angry person, but there was one man who brought out such emotions in her and Mac didn't have to ask which Neanderthal she was referring to.

"What's going on now?" Mac asked, trying to keep his frustration from coming through.

"I started talking to Carter again—"

"Oh, Laney," Mac groaned. "Are you kidding me?"

"Anyway," she continued, ignoring his protest. "Suddenly Carter calls and tells me he can't see me anymore. You guys may not like him, but my personal life is not your concern. We had a rough patch and I was going to give him another chance."

Actually, it was very much their concern, but he wasn't getting into that now. Having Laney as a baby sister was exhausting at times, but they usually handled her by going behind her back to keep her safe. Mac wouldn't let any harm come to her as long as he was alive, and he knew full well Braden felt the same way, as did Ryker, even though he was only a friend of the family.

"And how does Ryker come into play?"

Laney laughed. "Seriously? He obviously called Carter and said something to him. We were supposed to go out tonight for the first time since we broke up and Carter was adamant he couldn't see me again."

Mac shrugged, even though she couldn't see him. If Carter was scared off that easily then he didn't deserve Laney. End of story and good riddance.

"Listen, Carter isn't a good fit for you," Mac started as he glanced back into the restaurant and met Jenna's eyes. "You deserve someone who will put you above everything else and be completely loyal."

"Maybe Carter was that person," she retorted.

Something flashed in Jenna's eyes before she turned her attention back to whatever her sister was saying. A punch of reality hit him in the gut. From here on out he had to do right by Jenna. She trusted him, only him, to come to her rescue. If someone ever set out to "help" his sister by means of seduction, Mac would rip him limb from limb.

How could he seduce her when she'd placed her heart, her protection in his hands? The answer was as simple as it was complex…he couldn't.

"We went to great lengths to get Carter out of your life when you needed us to step in," Mac went on as he took a few more steps down the dock and away from a couple who had just come outside. "Even if Ryker did call Carter to scare him off, then you need to realize he has your best interests at heart."

"He doesn't have a heart."

That was debatable, but still. Mac wasn't going to keep arguing. "You need to settle this with Ryker."

"He won't take my calls."

"He's working on a lead." He didn't need to say what for. They'd all been diligently searching for the scrolls since their father had made them promise to uncover them. "Don't take it personally."

"If you called him he'd answer," she muttered. "If that jackass thinks he can avoid me…"

Mac smiled. "I'm sure he'll return your call soon enough. I need to get back to dinner."

"Sorry. I know you're with Jenna. Tell her I said hi."

"Will do. Love you, Laney."

"Love you, brother."

Mac shoved the phone back in his pocket and made a mental note to contact Ryker tomorrow. Laney was an adult, yes, but she was beautiful, and as the only female O'Shea, some men saw her as a challenge. Like hell.

"Everything okay?"

Mac jerked around. "Yeah. My sister said to tell you hi."

Jenna's face softened. "I haven't seen her since she came down to Miami to visit you."

Mac slipped his arm around her shoulders. "Let's get back to dinner."

Jenna paused, her hand on his chest as she looked up at him. "If we could hurry and pretend we can't wait to get back to the room that would be great."

Mac swallowed at the thought of her in a rush to get him alone, but he quickly reminded himself he'd vowed to cool it and respect her during their charade. But he had a feeling that keeping that vow would test every ounce of his willpower and sanity.

"Martin just came in and sat at another table, but I want out of here before you blacken his other eye."

Mac kissed her forehead. "No more punching tonight, I promise."

Jenna patted his chest and laughed. "You're all heart. My sister is pressing for more wedding details, so we need to keep the conversation on something else."

"Not a problem." He'd discuss the damn weather before he got into a conversation about his impending nuptials. That day would never come and even in theory, the idea made him cringe.

As they neared the table again, Mac slid his hand along Jenna's neck, smoothing her hair aside. "I hope you're ready to put on a show to make this believable. We've still got that bet on the line."

Jenna froze beneath his touch, but quickly recovered enough to throw him a killer smile. "I think you need to get ready for my performance."

Mac nipped at her lips and pulled her close. "Baby, I'm always ready."

Seven

Amy was saying something about... Jenna honestly had no clue because Mac had scooted so close to her. His hand was traveling up her thigh, pulling the hem of her dress up, and he'd just whispered something so naughty in her ear, she wondered where he learned of such a thing.

If his intent was to get her flustered and squirming in her seat, mission accomplished.

Jenna tipped her head just slightly, suppressing a groan as Mac's fingertips made a pattern over her bare skin. If he moved his hand any higher she'd have a hard time remaining ladylike in public.

Damn that man. He was owning this role of fiancé/lover. No way would he win this bet, though.

Jenna smiled and nodded as Amy stated how their mother had found the most beautiful lilac dress for the wedding. But Mac's relentless touches had her shifting in her seat, spreading her legs slightly and letting out a low, soft sigh.

Mac froze a half second before he moved his hand to her inner thigh. Jenna's first thought was that he'd probably never felt a thick, bare leg like hers before. Her second thought was…she wished he could just go a little higher to relieve her ache.

"If you did a Christmas wedding, we could totally do a classy white theme," Amy went on, clearly oblivious to what was happening beneath the table.

Unable to help herself, Jenna leaned against Mac. She told herself she was just playing the part, but she was starting to think this part was playing her. He removed his hand from her thigh, and she nearly whimpered at the loss, but then he smoothed her hair away from her neck and started massaging the sensitive flesh there. Oh, yeah. He had some talented hands and she didn't want to think about how many women had groaned beneath his touch.

"No matter when Jenna decides to have the wedding, she'll be a beautiful bride."

Mac kissed her cheek and trailed his fingertips down her spine, sending an instant onslaught of goose bumps all over her body despite the heat.

"I hate to cut this dinner short," Mac went on. "But Martin is staring in this direction and I won't have him upsetting Jenna again. Besides, I want to have as much alone time with my gorgeous fiancée as I can. You understand, don't you, Nathan?"

Nathan nodded and lifted his nearly empty beer mug. "I do. I'll talk to Martin in a bit. I didn't know he was harassing you guys."

"He's not harassing us." Jenna refused to add fuel to the fire. The situation with Martin was bad enough. "He just thinks we're getting back together and I've had to tell him several times it's not happening. I'm sure now that he's seen how close Mac and I are, he'll back off."

Mac squeezed her shoulder. "Let's go, sweetheart. I'm done discussing your ex."

The endearment he delivered seemed so genuine, so perfect. Jenna didn't want to get so wrapped up in this that she forgot what was truly happening. Mac was simply playing a role. He wasn't a man she could ever tame and he wasn't looking for anything beyond this week. She knew him better than most, so to cling to any false hope would only leave her with a bruised heart.

Amy winked at Jenna. "See you tomorrow. Don't forget we have a bonfire on the beach at nine."

Jenna came to her feet when Mac pulled out her chair. "I'll be there," she promised. "See you guys tomorrow."

Mac rested his hand on the small of her back, his fingertips brushing her rear end, sending even more jolts of arousal through her. She didn't remember being so responsive before, but she'd also never been touched so intimately by Mac, either. Clearly the man had a special touch, one her body instantly loved.

As soon as they reached the doorway, Mac patted her bottom. "Go on ahead, sweetheart. I'm going to settle the bill and I'll be right there."

"There's no bill," she told him. "It's all part of the package my sister paid for."

"Go on, Jenna."

Something about the way his eyes seemed darker, his smile seemed tighter, had her wondering what he wasn't telling her, but Jenna nodded and headed back toward their bungalow. She needed a moment without Mac, a moment away from his touch, his powerful presence. Jenna pulled in deep breaths as she walked along the docks leading toward various areas of the resort. If she ever did get married, she'd seriously consider Bora Bora for her honeymoon.

If she ever found the one who made her heart kick up, who made her want to rip his clothes off, who made her want to reveal all her hopes and fears. Did that miracle man even exist?

Well, Mac did all those things, but he'd made it abundantly clear he couldn't be that man. As soon as she entered her bungalow, she slid out of her wedges and padded across the room and out onto her private deck. She sank down onto the hammock and carefully swiveled around to lie back. The gentle breeze had her swaying. Jenna laced her hands over her abdomen and closed her eyes. Yeah, she'd definitely bring her husband here.

She let the daydream of a faceless man flood her mind. Would they make love out here in the open, but where nobody could see them? Would they walk hand in hand along the shore and discuss their dreams for the future? Have a romantic dinner and come back to their bungalow and skinny-dip in the dark?

"That must be some daydream."

Jenna jerked at Mac's voice.

"That was the sexiest smile I've ever seen."

When Jenna started to sit up, Mac put a hand on her back. "Don't get up," he told her as he leaned against the side of the bungalow and propped his foot up.

"You look so relaxed, I hate to disturb you." His mouth spread into a wide, toe-curling grin. "Now, tell me what put that smile on your face. Or should I say who?"

"Nobody in particular," she replied with a shrug. Jenna settled back down onto the woven ropes of the hammock and sighed. "Just thinking of bringing my future husband back here for our honeymoon. It's too romantic and gorgeous not to."

When he didn't respond, Jenna risked a glance. His eyes held hers, a muscle ticking in his jaw as he crossed his arms over that broad chest.

"Do you really have your mother's dress in storage?" he asked.

Swallowing, Jenna nodded. "Yeah. It's satin with a simple lace overlay. Her marriage may have been a disaster, but I love the vintage dress and it was still my mother's. It's perfect for me if I ever find the right man."

Perfect because Jenna had inherited her mother's curves and the measurements were just right. Amy had a different father and got her athletic build from him... lucky girl.

"What else would you want in your dream wedding?" he asked.

Jenna stared at him for a second before she laughed, shook her head and turned back to focus on the water just beyond their private deck. "Does it matter? Or is this another ploy for you to seduce me?"

"If I wanted to seduce you, I'd have already succeeded," he told her. "You know I want you physically, any man would be blind and a fool not to. But you were right. We're best friends and at the end of the week, that's what we still need to be."

Great. She was right. He was finally seeing reason. So why did she feel like she'd lost out on a once-in-a-lifetime opportunity?

"I won't lie," he went on. "You're still one of the sexiest women I've ever known, but I respect you, respect what we have."

Wait a second. She was one of the sexiest women he knew? Now he was just being kind, but she wasn't about to say anything because she wasn't one of those women who went fishing for compliments.

"You talked to Martin after I walked away didn't you?" she asked, already knowing the answer.

"I'm done talking about your ex," Mac replied, which told her all she needed to know. "Are you going to work on those flowers tonight? I can go pack more in if you need me to."

Jenna smiled. "You want to help put together wedding arrangements? I knew you had a soft side."

Mac grumbled. "I'm just offering to do some grunt work. Don't read too much into it."

Jenna needed a breather and she had to get these arrangements made. "Fine. Go bring me the rest of the lilacs and half of the greenery."

With a mock bow, Mac gave her a wink. "Consider it done."

Even when he was being a sarcastic goof, he made her heart flutter. She couldn't afford the flutter, the bundle of nerves or the tingles from his kisses.

At dinner, Martin hadn't come over to speak, so perhaps they were making headway. Maybe seeing her with Mac over and over would get through to him—or maybe Mac's fist helped. As much as she wasn't a fan of violence, she also knew Mac was effective when he wanted to be.

She recalled a time he'd been more than forceful at a party when a guy had hit on her and she'd politely turned down his advances. Unfortunately that guy hadn't taken no for an answer and Mac intervened. A slam against the wall and a threat she hadn't been able to overhear sent that guy packing in the other direction.

Mac was definitely a man she wanted in her corner... too bad she couldn't risk having him in her bed.

Mac's cell vibrated in his pocket just as he hit the entrance to the lobby of the resort. Glancing at the screen, he darted to the side of the building and slid his finger to answer the call.

"Ryker. What do you have?"

"Nothing yet on the scrolls, but we have a problem."

Not what Mac wanted to hear. He was having enough problems trying to remain on the strictly friend level with Jenna. Throwing in a dose of family issues wasn't going to help his mood.

"It's Shane," Ryker went on.

Shane, Braden's nemesis and all-round world-class ass. He'd tried to ruin their family years ago when a business deal had gone sour. He'd attempted to sic the authorities on Patrick, who'd still been running the show. Only Shane hadn't been smart enough to realize the commissioner, the police chief and the FBI director were in the O'Sheas' back pocket. Poor Shane, rookie mistake.

"What the hell is he doing now?"

"I have no clue who is feeding him information, but he's been following me for two days."

Mac glanced around to make sure nobody could hear him. "What the hell does he want?"

"No idea," Ryker stated. "He's trying to be sneaky, but I spotted him when I got to my hotel. I had Laney check into his travel arrangements, and he has an open-ended airline ticket. He's also staying in my hotel. Laney made things a bit difficult for him by hacking into his bank account and moving his funds around."

Mac ran a hand over his face. His sister, the computer hacker. She'd be dangerous if they gave her too much leeway.

"Did you call Braden?"

The cell rustled on the other end before Ryker's reply came through, his tone hushed as if he were worried about being overheard. "He texted me yesterday and said not to bother him unless I found the scrolls. Claimed something about a personal problem with Zara. I didn't ask any more."

Mac frowned. He'd gotten a text from Braden telling him there was a slight issue at home, but it was nothing for Mac to worry about. What was going on?

"That's not all," Ryker went on. "Laney received a threat from Shane through her email. He tried to encrypt it, but she was able to trace it back to him."

Mac gripped the phone. Nobody threatened his family and lived to follow through. "What did the message say?"

"She wouldn't tell me, but I could tell she was shaken up."

"It's not like her to be caught off guard," Mac stated. They'd never known any other way of life, so the contents of the email must have been pretty harsh.

"There's more," Ryker stated. "Someone tried to grab her as she went into a coffee shop two days ago. Luckily an off-duty cop was there and was able to stop it."

Mac's blood boiled. "Why the hell am I just now hearing about this?"

"Because I just heard about it," Ryker retorted. "Laney is smart. She's keeping low and staying home with her security alarm on, but she finally told me when I called her to check on another matter."

Braden may want this family to go legit, but there were times that extreme measures were called for.

"Shane has been a thorn in our side for years," Ryker

went on. "Now he's literally threatening one of our own. I know that was him who tried to grab her because she said the guy had a mask on, but it slipped. She saw the tattoo on his neck. I don't care that he's following me. I can handle him, but Laney is another matter. When are we going to end this once and for all?"

Mac rubbed a hand down his face and blew out a breath. Damn it, he hated making this call. Braden had been adamant about moving this family in a new direction since their father had passed. No more killings. That was Braden's main stance, but Shane had crossed the line by threatening Laney. "Wait," Mac stated. "Braden really wants O'Shea's to make a new start and I can't say as I blame him. He's got a fiancée to think of now and he's in charge. Let's try to get ahold of him again and see what he thinks. If we can't contact him, I'll make a decision."

Ryker sighed. "Fine. But if Shane gets in my way or tries to thwart my plans regarding the scrolls, I'm not backing down. And if I even think he's contacted Laney again, I won't ask for permission to proceed."

Mac gripped his phone tighter. "Make sure you call or text me before you do anything."

Ryker grunted and hung up. As Mac slid his phone back into his pocket, he thought back to all Shane had done. Braden had practiced serious restraint a few months ago when Shane had been harassing Zara. Apparently Zara and Shane had gone out a few times, and once Zara had showed interest in Braden, Shane took that as a personal slap in the face. His pathetic attempt at making their lives hell backfired, but Shane was lucky he was still on this side of the grave.

Mac tried Braden's cell, but got no answer. What on earth could be so dire at home that Braden had checked out? That wasn't like him, especially as the new head of the family. He took that role seriously. Worry slid through Mac as he shot off a quick text asking if everything was all right. Once he knew what Braden's status was, he'd delve into the mess with Shane because Laney's very life could be on the line.

Pulling in a breath and trying to focus on the task Jenna had sent him out for, Mac turned back toward the lobby. If Braden continued to be unreachable and Shane forced their hand, Mac wouldn't be able to hold Ryker back much longer.

And, in all honesty, Mac wasn't so sure he wanted to. Legitimacy be damned.

Eight

"I really need to get back to working on the flowers."

Not bothering to even slow down, Mac laced his fingers with Jenna's and kept walking down the beach. "You didn't come to bed until three this morning because you were working."

Well, that was true, but she'd also been avoiding going to bed because she was having a difficult time lying there beside such temptation. The fewer hours the better. The warmth of his body next to hers was something she could get used to and that was a major problem.

"I have yet to start on the largest arrangements and the wedding is in three days."

She risked a glance to see if he was going to respond, but he just kept walking in that sexy, I've-got-all-the-time-in-the-world kind of way. Without a shirt. With all those glorious, tanned muscles clenching with each step and strut.

And he was totally oblivious to the fact that he stole her breath and made her heart quicken.

Jenna blinked and focused on looking ahead. While Mac had all the confidence in the world, she tugged on her strapless cover-up once more to avoid a wardrobe malfunction. Mac had suggested they head to the beach to "be seen" so she'd thrown on the only bathing suit she'd packed, because it was the only one she owned. Clearly swimwear was designed by the devil and a host of supermodels.

The cover-up helped, though. As long as she kept her shield in place, she didn't feel so…exposed.

"Stop fidgeting," he commanded. "You look fine."

Great. She looked fine and he looked delicious.

"C'mon," he said, tugging her toward the water's edge. "Let's cool off."

Jenna pulled her hand free. "Go ahead. I'll just sit here."

She sank onto the sand, shoving her toes into the warmth. When Mac stood in front of her, blocking the sun, she eased back on her hands and stared up at him.

"Come in the water with me."

"I'm fine," she told him. "Go on ahead."

When he took a seat next to her, Jenna continued to stare out at the ocean through the tinted lenses of her sunglasses. They'd only seen one other couple walking along the beach. It was still early and the weather was perfect. Everything about Bora Bora, this wedding, the ambiance, was perfect. What wasn't perfect was the turmoil rolling inside her. Maybe Martin had gotten the hint and was going to leave her alone. Maybe she and Mac didn't have to be quite so touchy-feely in public.

Because her body still tingled from the table experience.

Mac's hand brushed along her shoulder, smoothing her hair away from her back and over the other shoulder. "Take off the cover-up, Jenna."

Stiffening beneath his touch, letting his husky words wash over her, Jenna's refusal was on the tip of her tongue.

"I know you're not comfortable," he went on, his tone low and soft. "But you're one sexy woman. You're made like women should be, Jen. All those curves."

He palmed her back as he leaned in closer. "You make a man think of things he shouldn't."

A shiver racked her body. "You're delusional."

"No, I'm honest."

Jenna glanced his way, her hair falling over her shoulder, the ends tickling her bare thigh. "You don't need to say pretty words, Mac. I only needed you to pretend."

Mac jerked off his sunglasses, then hers, and looked her dead in the eye. "You think I'm just saying this to make you feel good? I've always thought you were sexy, Jenna. That's never been a question."

Yeah, well, clothes could camouflage quite a bit.

Mac slid his hand down, his fingers curling around the elastic on the top of her cover-up. Jenna jerked.

"Don't," he ordered. "Let me."

Closing her eyes, she waited for him to pry her security blanket down. She hated this. Hated knowing she would be exposed in seconds. No, she'd never worn a swimsuit around him. She rarely put a suit on, period. Why was he doing this? To prove he could?

"Mac." Her plea came out as a whisper.

The material slid over her breasts and down her torso, and Jenna sat up, wrapping her arms around her waist in some vain attempt to keep herself covered.

"Lift your hips," he said, continuing to pull the material down.

In no time, he slid the cover-up down her bare legs and tossed it to the side. Jenna clenched her teeth, blinking back the burn of tears threatening to spill.

"Look at me."

Jenna pulled in a breath and turned to Mac. As he kept his eyes on hers, he gently eased her arms away from her body. "Hiding such beauty should be a crime."

When he said these things in such a convincing way, Jenna believed him. Mac kept secrets regarding his business at times, but he'd never flat-out lied to her face. Was he being sincere? Why did this tender moment feel so intimate, so raw and...real?

"I'm a heavy girl," she told him, still holding his gaze. "I know what I look like in a suit, Mac."

"If you know how stunning, sexy and intriguing you look, then we're on the same page." His smile nearly killed her. He wasn't mocking, he was flirting.

Mac. The good-time guy with a mysterious side.

When he smoothed his hand over her knee and up her thigh, Jenna tensed again.

"Wh-what are you doing?" she asked.

With a shrug, his eyes darted to where his hand traveled across her skin. "Being affectionate. What if someone is watching? What if someone can see us, but we can't see them?"

Right. The charade. But as his fingertips continued their path up and down her bare leg, Mac leaned in and kissed her shoulder.

"Mac—"

"Jenna," he murmured against her skin.

He kissed her again, higher on her shoulder this time, and Jenna couldn't stop the instinctive reaction as she tipped her head to the side, silently pleading for more of his touch.

Whatever he was doing felt absolutely amazing. For right now, she didn't care if someone was watching, she didn't care if she was sitting here in only her plain, old, black, one-piece suit. What she did care about was how Mac made her feel beautiful with his touch, with words that were from his heart.

When he slid his hand from her leg, up over her stomach, she stiffened slightly until he kept going. Continuing his trail over her breast, her collarbone and finally her jaw, Mac turned her face toward his and captured her mouth.

Jenna would never get used to this. Each time he kissed her, all three times now, seemed like the first. Nerves swirled around in her stomach, excitement and arousal kicked into high gear and she completely lost all touch with reality. Mac knew what he was doing and he knew he could kiss her anytime he wanted.

No, she didn't want to get hurt at the end of all of this, but she couldn't tell him no right now, either. Call her a masochist, she didn't care. How could she care about anything when Mac's hand slid into her hair, his other hand wrapping around her waist as he shifted his body and leaned into her?

Jenna laid a hand on his chest to steady herself. That hard muscle beneath her palm had her curling her fingertips into him, wanting more, greedily trying to take it.

Mac's lips slid over hers. There was so much power, so much dominance radiating from him. The complete and utter control on his part was a turn-on…something she never thought she'd be attracted to.

"Let me take you back to the bungalow," he muttered

against her lips. "Let's finish what we started the other night."

He tipped her head back, kissing a path along her jawline, then back toward her ear. That warm breath sent shivers racing all over her body.

"My word. You two are heating up the beach."

Jenna jerked away from Mac, but he kept his hold around her waist and threw a smile over her shoulder. Her mother's elated tone had Jenna cringing.

"Good morning, Mary."

Seriously? Did this not faze him at all? They'd been caught making out by her mother and he was acting as if they'd run into each other in the milk aisle at the grocery store.

Jenna twisted, eyed her cover-up mere feet away and glanced at her mother. "Morning, Mom."

Her mother's crooked grin spoke volumes.

"You two may want to head back to your bungalow," she said with a wink. "Young love can be a bit spontaneous, can't it?"

"That it can," Mac agreed.

He stood and extended a hand to help Jenna up. She grabbed her cover-up and let Mac pull her to her feet. Jenna held the material in front of her as she stared back at her still-smiling mother.

"I didn't get to see you yesterday," Jenna said, hoping this encounter wasn't as awkward as it was feeling.

"I heard you went to dinner with Amy and Nathan. I love that my girls have found two wonderful men who clearly make them so happy."

Jenna swallowed the lump of guilt as Mac slid his arm around her waist and pulled her closer to his side. The support he silently gave her was humbling. He was always giving, especially a few moments ago when he'd been ready to give her himself.

But that was not a thought she could entertain right now.

"Well, don't let me keep you two," Mary went on, waving her hand. "I need to finish my morning walk and then head to my massage. I may never leave this place."

Jenna instantly found herself wrapped in her mother's arms. "You look so happy, darling," her mom whispered in her ear before pulling away. Mary squeezed Jenna's shoulders and blinked back tears. "This is exactly the life I wanted for you. A strong man who will treat you right. Both of my girls are settling down."

Quickly, Jenna pasted a smile on her face, keeping up with the farce that had snowballed out of control.

After one more quick hug, Mary pulled away and patted Mac on the shoulder. "You're perfect for her."

As her mother made her way down the beach, Jenna wrestled into her cover-up, keeping her back to Mac who hadn't said a word. She suddenly felt awful. This wasn't right. None of it.

But as soon as she turned, that desire in Mac's eyes was still evident and she couldn't be strong enough for both of them because if he so much as touched her again, she didn't know that she could say no. She'd nearly proven that point moments ago.

Would she have gone back to the bungalow if her mother hadn't shown up? Would she and Mac be making love right now?

No. Because they weren't in love. He loved women in general and she refused to be just another proverbial notch.

"I need to get back to work," she said, skirting around

him. Making a quick, classy getaway on sand wasn't the easiest of moves, but Jenna forced herself to keep going.

As she made her way to the dock that led to the walkways to various bungalows, Jenna sensed Mac right behind her. She didn't slow down, couldn't turn and look at him right now. Honestly, she wanted to be left alone, but no doubt Mac would march right in behind her and make some argument for why they should give into their now-obvious desire for each other. Something about acting on emotions and consenting adults and such.

But his heart wasn't on the line. Jenna couldn't keep letting herself get close to Mac or she would find herself crushed at the end of the week, when they returned to Miami as friends.

As she entered the bungalow, she knew she had to put to the brakes on this. Just as she was able to catch her breath, Mac stepped through the door. Only a few feet from him, Jenna concentrated on his face and not the bare chest still exposed, still casting out too much temptation.

"This has to stop," she stated. "I can't do it anymore."

Mac crossed his arms, shifting his stance. "Don't be afraid of what happened, Jenna. I'm trying to keep my promise to you and play this part, but damn it, I'm having a difficult time keeping things G-rated."

Said the man who rotated women with the slightest shift in the wind's direction. To Jenna what they'd just shared was…special.

He'd gotten her out of her cover-up; he'd shown her how beautiful she was with very few words. She knew he wasn't just trying to seduce her. Mac cared for her and wouldn't hurt her like that, but he had no clue how fast she was falling for him. If he did, he would be on his jet before she could say "best friend."

"This isn't a game," she cried. "I thought I could distance myself from all of this emotionally. I thought I could pretend, but I can't. It's too much."

The muscle in his jaw clenched. "If you want me to leave, say the word."

His eyes held hers and Jenna saw a flash of hurt there. Jenna didn't want to think she had the power to hurt him. Mac was a force of nature, he was strong, much stronger than she was when it came to personal matters.

But he stared at her, waiting for her reply, and she only had one option.

"You should go."

Nine

"Honey, you're late."

Because I didn't want to come.

Jenna pasted on a smile and shrugged. "Sorry, Mom. I got caught up in the flower arrangements taking over my kitchen."

Mary glanced around and Jenna knew what was coming next. Cringing, she waited.

"Where's Mac?"

"He wasn't feeling well." The lie slid easily off her tongue. And it was that ease of lying to her mother's face that had Jenna needing this farce to come to an end. "Let's join the others."

Jenna slid her arm through her mother's and steered her toward the bonfire already in full swing. A beach party with music, laughter and what appeared to be enough food for a small village was exactly the distraction Jenna needed.

Spotting her, Martin immediately pulled one of the bridesmaids off to the side, no doubt to feed her some line of BS…poor girl. But if that meant he was leaving Jenna alone, who was she to complain?

It was a perfect evening. The warm breeze from the ocean felt amazing and a small band was playing some tropical tunes that blended romance and fun. Her sister had definitely gone all out with her budget, but Amy's defense had been that she only planned on marrying once so she was going big.

"The fresh pineapple is heaven," her mother commented. "You have to get a plate of food. Those kabobs with glazed chicken… I have no clue what the chef did, but I need that recipe."

Jenna half listened as her mother discussed the varieties of food available. She really wasn't in the mood to eat, wasn't in the mood to party. She'd been hoping that once she got here she would perk up, but all she kept seeing was Mac's face as he'd walked out of the bungalow. She'd hurt him. Knowing she even had that ability was crippling because she loved him. Loved the friend he always was, and was starting to love the man.

The shaky ground she walked on could crumble at any moment and where would that leave her? Falling face-first into a sea of humiliation and heartache.

"I'm actually not that hungry," she told her mother as she took a step back. "If you'll excuse me a minute, I want to find Amy and ask about the arrangements."

"Of course, dear. She was talking with Nathan and the caterer right before you got here, but I don't see her now."

Jenna patted her mother's arm. "I'll find her. Go dance and have fun. You look beautiful tonight."

Mary's smile widened. "You're sweet. Please, don't

feel you have to stay all evening. If Mac isn't feeling well, go back to him."

Go back to him. If he were actually hers, she never would have left his side.

"He'll be fine," Jenna assured her mom as she turned and headed in the other direction. At least she'd told her mom the truth. Mac would be fine. He was always fine.

But Jenna wondered where he'd gone. When he left he hadn't taken his stuff, but she hadn't seen him for several hours. Maybe he was waiting until she was gone to come get his things? She had no idea, but as soon as she got back, she was going to text him. She'd tried a few minutes ago and he hadn't responded yet. She couldn't handle this tension, the conflict she'd single-handedly placed between them.

Jenna smiled and said her hellos as she passed by the familiar faces from the wedding party. Amy's best friend from college, her best friend from grade school and her husband. Everyone was here for a good time and Jenna wasn't about to put a damper on her sister's big moment. The pity party could come later, when Jenna was back in her bungalow alone with the pint of ice cream she'd requested from the kitchen.

Jenna didn't care if sobbing into ice cream made her a cliché. She'd made her best friend pretend to be her lover and it had gone horribly wrong, so bring on the clichés and bring on the spoon because she was ready to dive into that container of Rocky Road.

"You look stunning tonight."

Jenna jerked around to see Martin standing way too close for her comfort. How had he sneaked up on her? Oh, yeah, she'd been busy plotting her evening of gluttony.

She resisted the urge to adjust her halter-style dress. "I'm looking for Amy."

Just as she turned to leave, Martin grabbed her arm. He didn't squeeze or use force, but she didn't want his hands on her.

Her eyes dropped to where he held her, then up to meet his gaze. "Let go."

"I just want a minute to talk now that your goon isn't around." He let his hand fall back to his side. "Can you give me two minutes?"

Jenna let out a laugh as she squared her shoulders and crossed her arms. "Two minutes? You think that will be enough time to undo the damage? Because I could give you two months to grovel and I still wouldn't forgive you or take you back."

Martin shook his head as he ran a hand through his blond hair. "I'm human, Jenna. I made a mistake."

"I'm human, too, but I wouldn't purposely hurt someone I care about."

And the second the words left her mouth, she realized she'd just told one more lie. What kind of person had she turned into? All to get Martin to stay away. How was that working out for her? Because Mac was gone and Martin was less than a foot away.

"Let me make it up to you," he pleaded. "You don't want to marry an O'Shea. You know what they say about that family. I put up with you being his friend, but I can't stand by and let you marry him."

Martin's eyes darted over her shoulder, then widened. Immediately Jenna knew who stood behind her. She tensed because Martin was still sporting the evidence of Mac's rage.

"Oh, don't let me stop you," Mac stated. Did he sound... amused? "I'd like to hear more of these rumors regarding my family and how you can't let Jenna marry me."

Standing directly between them, Jenna kept her back

to Mac. Hopefully she wouldn't have to become the human shield between these two.

"We're having a private conversation," Martin stated.

Mac's hands curled around Jenna's bare shoulders. "When you're talking to my girl, you're not allowed privacy. So, please, don't let me stop this speech because I'm sure you rehearsed it."

Tension seemed to envelop them, blocking them off from the cheerful party, the upbeat music and the laughter. It was more than Jenna could handle.

"Go, Martin. Before this gets worse. Just…go."

His eyes held hers, he opened his mouth as if he wanted to say something more, but finally wised up and turned away. Jenna remained still, waiting for Mac to say something, to remove his hands or…she didn't know what, but she didn't want to make the first move.

When he seemed content to stay just as he was, Jenna sighed. "What are you doing here?" she whispered.

"I told you I'd be here for you this week." He brushed her hair aside. Seconds later his lips grazed her ear. "I never go back on a promise, Jenna."

At the contact, chills covered her body. "I'm not sure I can keep this up."

"Are you saying I won the bet?" he asked, a hint of humor to his voice. "Because I'm ready to call in my favor."

Jenna shook her head and turned. "No. I'm not saying you won the bet. There's more to this than some silly bet we placed."

The humor vanished from his face. "For the next few minutes, we're in love. Whatever else we need to discuss can wait until we're alone. Deal?"

Jenna nodded and blew out a breath. "Deal."

Mac wrapped his arms around her, pulling her directly into his warm embrace. "I was never going to walk away," he whispered in her ear. "I only left to give you the space you needed. I would never desert you."

Tears pricked her eyes, emotions clogged her throat. Jenna nodded against his chest because words were not coming to her.

"Oh, you're feeling better."

Her mother's elated voice cut into the moment and Jenna cringed. Would Mac grasp the fact that Jenna had lied to cover for him?

"I wouldn't miss this party," he replied easily, sliding Jenna around to the crook of his side. "Sorry I'm late."

Mary waved a hand in the air. "Don't worry about it. I'm just so glad you could join us. Jenna looks happier than she did when I first saw her."

Mac threw Jenna a heavy-lidded glance. "I'll make sure she's always happy."

The promise in his eyes, the conviction in those words gave Jenna a false sense of hope. Once again. He couldn't possibly know what she was battling within. He couldn't have any idea how much she wanted him to be serious, to be saying these things as a man who was falling in love.

But Mac O'Shea didn't fall—in business or in love. He remained in charge, flitting from one moment to the next without a care in the world.

As if to solidify his statement, Mac kissed her. Nothing too intimate, just his lips to hers. A soft promise. A gentle understanding that he was a man of his word.

Yet, as plain and simple as his kiss was, Jenna felt as if she was twisted even tighter in his web. Despite her telling him to leave, he'd come back for her. He had nothing to gain by being here. Everything he'd done in the past three days was for her.

How could she not fall in love with a man who made

her feel so special, put her first in his life and made her toes curl with the simplest of touches?

Those were some very good questions. Too bad she had none of the answers.

Ten

Mac stood on the edge of the dock, staring out at the inky water. They'd stayed at the bonfire well past midnight. For the requisite toast, Jenna had opted to have a glass of wine. He'd never seen her drink because of her mother's past alcoholism. Mary had been clean for several years now and she'd not batted an eyelash when the wine was brought out. She was a strong woman; she'd raised strong daughters.

But the glass of wine on Jenna's empty stomach had made her woozy and she'd clung to him all the way home.

Home. Ridiculous to think of this little structure on stilts in the water as home. Even more ridiculous to think of living with Jenna as *home*.

Once they'd returned, Mac had showered quickly to rid himself of the bonfire's smoky scent. When he'd come out, Jenna had been pouring a glass of juice.

She'd downed that glass and headed to the shower.

Mac had waited outside the bathroom door until she was done. The last thing he needed was her falling and hitting her head because she wasn't used to alcohol.

Now he stood out on the deck, as far away from temptation as he could handle. Jenna was proving to be more of a problem than he'd originally thought. Well, she wasn't necessarily the problem, but his unwanted emotions were. Over and over he told himself to leave her alone, to stop all the touching and kissing, but then he got near her and all of that logic vanished, quickly replaced by hormones.

Bare feet shuffled behind him and he forced himself to remain still. She was tipsy, no doubt vulnerable, and the last thing she needed was flirty advances from him. When she'd sent him away earlier, he'd promised himself when he came back he'd be on his best behavior. That hadn't lasted long.

But he couldn't forget the image of Jenna's face when he'd arrived at the bonfire. She'd truly been shocked that he'd come back. Had she honestly thought he wouldn't be there for her? What type of men had she been dating?

"My father left my mother when Amy and I were younger."

Her soft words slid over him and he knew she was about to let him into that part of her world he'd never seen. After years of friendship, he truly knew nothing about her father...only that the man wasn't in the picture. Mac also knew Jenna and Amy had different fathers, but everything else he knew about Jenna was from events he'd been present for over the past decade.

"Apparently he'd been cheating on her for some time," Jenna went on. "Mom had no clue. She'd been so in love. She would have dinner ready when he came home from work. She'd iron his clothes and have them ready. She was always hugging him or laughing at his lame jokes. I saw the love in her eyes."

Mac didn't like the sorrow in Jenna's tone, but he wasn't about to stop her now. He needed to see inside her life in order to understand her better. But maybe she didn't want him to know all of this.

"Is this a drunk confession?" he asked, only half joking.

"I'm not drunk." Jenna laughed. "Okay, maybe a little tipsy, but I know full well what I'm telling you."

Mac turned to face her and an instant punch of lust hit him hard. She leaned against the door frame, casual as you please, wearing a short, strapless dress that clung to her damp skin. Her wet hair lay perfectly over one shoulder. The glistening droplets covering her body caught the moonlight with each breath she took and it was all Mac could do to stand still and not go touch her.

"My mother was devastated when my dad left." Jenna's arms came up, wrapping around her midsection. "She was completely blindsided and the bastard left her a note. He was such a coward. He left a note to a woman who was so in love with him she would've done anything he asked. He left two little girls who had to grow up too fast and learn the harsh realities of life and marriage."

The hitch in her voice gutted him. She'd dreamed of a wedding, she'd kept her mother's wedding dress. Clearly she believed she'd find "the one" despite all she'd witnessed as a young girl.

His Jenna had hopes and dreams, and he was riding a fine line of destroying everything. He knew she was getting attached. He could feel it in her touch, taste the emotion in her kisses.

"Amy and I had no clue how to help my mom," she went on, staring out into the night as if she were watching the events unfold before her. "She rarely got out of bed. When she did, it was to get a drink. Finally she started keeping the bottles by her bed. Amy would fix my hair for school and make sure to hold my hand as we went to the bus stop. Amy and I were pretty good at covering up the lack of parenting at our house until it came time for report cards and Amy forged my mom's signature."

Mac could easily see these two sisters looking after each other, and worrying for their mother who had been slapped in the face by fate's harsh hand.

"Long story short, our neighbors, who had kids our age, ended up taking us in while mom went to rehab." Jenna shook her head as if to clear her thoughts. "We don't talk about that time because it was so dark, so depressing and that's not who my mother is."

"That's why one glass of wine has you stumbling."

Jenna nodded. "I'll have a glass of wine every now and then, but I saw how it nearly destroyed my mother. I saw how falling for the wrong man crippled her to the point I didn't recognize her anymore."

And that's why she was fighting this attraction. Everything fell into place now. He'd vowed before not to touch her when he didn't have to, but now Mac knew he needed to be hands off unless they were in public and trying to keep up this charade.

Blowing out a frustrated breath, Mac moved to the hammock and eased down. Flipping his feet up, he reclined, lacing his hands behind his head.

"Go on to bed, Jenna. We've had a long day."

Silence filled the space, but she didn't move. He was hanging on by a thread here. As if he weren't physically attracted enough, now she went and threw vulnerability into the mix. He couldn't handle knowing she was hurting, but he only knew one way to console her. Having sex with her would be a temporary moment of happiness and once they were done, she'd hate him and he couldn't live with that.

Having Jenna hurt at his hands wasn't an option. This could never be just a fling for her and he should've accepted that from the beginning. Or, maybe in the back of his mind he *had* realized it, but didn't want to face the truth staring him in the face.

"Thank you for coming back," she murmured. "I thought you'd leave the island."

"I promised I'd be here for you, didn't I?"

"Yeah, but things are more intense than either of us intended."

Understatement of the year. And he was seriously rethinking his entire strategy.

"I'm sorry I hurt you earlier," she went on. "I'm not good at lying to people I love."

"A few more days and this will all be over."

"Will it?" she asked. "Because I'm not sure I can forget how you kissed me, how you've held me, touched me."

Shutting his eyes, he gritted his teeth and attempted to dig deep for willpower. If she'd told him this before her confession about her father, he would have been all over her. But now he knew why she was so leery and he knew he had to take a step back...even if it killed him.

"Can you forget?" she whispered.

"Leave it, Jenna. Go to bed."

"Where will you be?"

"Right here."

The second he heard her cross the deck, he froze. He opened his eyes to see her standing next to him, her gaze on his.

"You don't have to stay out here," she told him, her voice huskier than seconds ago. "Maybe I'm ready to give in. Maybe I'm ready to stop being so damn good all the time and holding out for the perfect man in my life."

"It's the wine," he told her. "In the morning you'll feel different."

He pulled his hands from behind his head and laid them on his abdomen. Those hands had done some ugly things, too many to even count, and he didn't deserve to have them on her body. He didn't deserve what she willingly offered.

"What if I don't feel different, Mac?" she asked. Those eyes of hers remained locked on to his and it was all he could do not to jerk her down on top of him and finish what she'd started.

"Go to bed, Jenna. Alone."

"Mac—"

"Damn it," he yelled, hating when she jumped. "You have no idea what you're saying. I don't do relationships, I do sex. That's it. I don't want more and I won't give more. We're friends. I shouldn't have taken it so far when we were alone, but you do things to me. I lost my head for a bit. I promise it won't happen again."

She bit down on her lip, crossing her arms in front of her chest. "You're a liar. You want me as much as I want you."

She was right. He was a liar. Millions of dollars rolled in from his ability to lie and cheat. He'd ordered killings and may again sooner rather than later. He didn't deserve this beautiful, sweet woman before him.

Mac eased up slightly on the swaying hammock and stared her straight in the eyes. "I can't want you. Not like that. Not anymore."

He heard her breath hitch, saw the shimmer in her eyes and he cursed himself. He'd never forgive himself if they were intimate and she fell for him. They'd go their separate ways in Miami and she'd be hurt. She couldn't be part of his life, not the ugly world he was born into. She'd be ruined and he hated like hell that Martin had been right.

With a tilt of her chin as she blinked back tears, Jenna took only a second to compose herself. "I never thought you'd turn into a coward."

"Coward?"

She leaned down, gripped the ropes on either side of him, sending the hammock swaying slightly. "You're afraid of wanting me for more than sex. You know it, and you're terrified because I know it."

Damn it, this was going too far. "Jenna—"

"Unless you're about to tell me I'm right, then save it." Her eyes narrowed as she licked her lips. Those lips he'd tasted, those same lips he craved when they weren't on his. "I'm going to bed alone. I don't care what you do anymore. If you can't be honest with me, then we have nothing more to say."

With a quick jerk he didn't see coming, she flipped the hammock and sent him plummeting face-first onto the deck. Mac turned his head just in time to see her bare feet disappear into the bungalow. The bedroom door slammed seconds later.

Mac couldn't help but laugh as he lay there on the hard floor. One glass of wine and his Jenna was aroused, angry and feisty.

Damn if that didn't make him want her more than ever.

Eleven

Jenna woke with a start when her pillow was jerked from beneath her head. Disoriented, she blinked against the bright sunlight streaming through her open blinds. Blinds she'd closed before bed.

Jenna turned her head to see Mac standing beside her bed, holding her beloved pillow.

"Whatever you're smirking about, go away and give me back my pillow."

His rich laughter flooded the room. "Get up, sunshine. Today we're getting back to Mac and Jenna. No wedding talk, no pretend relationship, just us."

Figuring she had no choice, and since she was already awake, Jenna sat up in her bed and rubbed her eyes. "What do you mean, back to us?"

He tossed her pillow behind her and took a seat on the edge of the bed, caging her legs in on either side with his hands. "I mean things have been too intense lately.

We need a break from this charade and I just want to be us again."

She couldn't agree more. One of them was going to break if they didn't step away from the emotional chaos that had been controlling them. But how could they just be themselves? They were on this island with a slew of wedding people, her mother and sister and Martin.

"What did you have in mind?" she asked.

"Just get dressed and meet me out front in five minutes."

Jenna laughed as Mac jumped off the bed and headed toward the door. "I'll need more than five minutes to throw clothes on and brush my teeth."

He gripped the edge of the door and threw her a look over his shoulder. "Fine. Seven minutes. No more."

Rolling her eyes, Jenna grabbed her pillow and tossed it across the room. Mac closed the door just in time.

Throwing her covers off, Jenna was out of bed in seconds flat. She got ready quicker than she would've liked, but with her hair up in a knot on her head, a simple tank sundress and clean teeth, this was as good as it was going to get. Who knew what Mac had planned? He was always acting on a whim, living from moment to moment.

Jenna was relieved he didn't bring up her blatant advances from last night. Perhaps whatever outing he had planned was a way to get them to move beyond this awkward, warped version of a fake engagement. She was too confused over what was going on, between what was real and what was completely fabricated, to keep up the pretense.

The bedroom door flew open just as she slid into her silver-sequined flip-flops.

"Oh, good. You're ready a minute early."

Jenna eyed her extremely anxious friend. "Am I going

to need a purse or my beach bag? A swimsuit? A little hint would be helpful."

"You look fine." He jerked his head. "Let's go."

With a shrug, she followed him out. She had no idea what he had planned, but she was more than ready for a break. Who knew she'd need a break from her fake boyfriend only a few days into the relationship? Perhaps she wasn't cut out for relationships of any kind.

Last night she'd nearly botched their friendship. How would this morning be playing out had Mac given in? Had they spent the night together, would he still be planning this surprise for her? Or would he have woken with regrets?

She shoved aside the what-ifs because, in reality, Mac was giving them a new start this morning. Maybe he was doing this so she didn't feel uncomfortable. Or maybe her throwing herself at him had meant nothing and this was just another day.

"You're frowning." Mac took her hand and led her down the dock. "Everything that happened before this morning has no place in your mind."

Jenna blinked against the sun. "Just tell me what we're doing."

He stopped, turned and offered her a smile that had her toes curling in her flip-flops. "We're going on a helicopter ride. We'll be away from the resort, nobody will be around, no cell phones, no fake relationships. Just Mac and Jenna."

"Sounds simple enough," she replied with a smile of her own. "I've never been in a helicopter."

Squeezing her hand, he headed to the end of the dock. "Then I'm happy to be your first."

Jenna leaned over and stared down at all the loveliness below. The lush, natural beauty, the sparkling water surrounding the small island. No buildings, no people. Absolutely breathtaking.

"I've never seen anything like this," she said into her headset. "I'm not sure I want to know how you managed to get a helicopter at your disposal. Not to mention the fact I didn't even know you could fly a helicopter."

Mac's rich laughter came through the earphones. "There's plenty you still don't know about me, Jenna. But you know the important stuff."

The important stuff. More like what he considered important. Still, she hadn't exactly opened up to him about her past…or the feelings that were overwhelming her now.

"Mac, look." She pointed to the breathtaking waterfall that came into view. "It's gorgeous."

Mac maneuvered the helicopter down closer. Jenna nearly plastered herself to the window as she watched the aqua water spill into a small, naturally made pool. The tropical plants surrounding the area seemed to invite only those who were lucky enough to find it.

As Mac took the helicopter even lower, Jenna turned to him. "I've never seen anything so stunning."

His eyes flickered to hers briefly. "I have," he murmured as he watched the controls. His words were so soft, so low, but she'd heard them loud and clear through the headset.

"What are you doing?" she asked as he hovered over the ground.

"Landing," he said matter-of-factly.

"Landing? Did you plan on bringing me here?"

With a shrug, he maneuvered the helicopter down on the ground and killed the engines. Finally, when he took off his own headphones, she did, too.

"Mac?"

A slow, easy smile slid over his face. "I knew this island was here. I wanted to show you, but I wasn't sure if we could land here or not."

Jenna squealed as she stepped from the chopper. "This is the coolest place ever."

Smoothing down her cotton dress, she tiptoed over the bright vegetation. The colors in all the blossoms and blooms were beyond overwhelming. She'd never seen anything like this.

Spinning in a circle, arms outstretched, she attempted to soak up all the beauty, to fully absorb everything all at once.

She caught Mac's smile as his eyes locked on to hers. "I knew you'd love this place," he told her. "I was hoping I could get you close enough because I found out there were plants and flowers here that are nearly nonexistent anywhere else in the world."

He knew her so well. He may buy jewels and fancy gifts for his arm candy, but Jenna knew their bond was too deep for such superficial things. When he wanted to surprise her, he went above and beyond.

"This is even better than the time you brought me a pint of Rocky Road and that terrible movie when I twisted my ankle."

She'd joined her local gym in an attempt to get healthier, but she'd tripped over the elliptical before she could even get on the darn thing. Jenna had taken that as a sign and never gone back.

"I'd say this surprise trumps that one," he agreed with a laugh. "Let's explore."

Mac held out his hand and as she placed her palm against his, she couldn't help but smile. The day was gorgeous, Mac was fighting to keep this relationship right where it should be. This is what they were. They were smiles and good times. They were surprises and last-minute planning. Well, he was last-minute; she preferred a spreadsheet.

"I can't believe you did this for me," she muttered as they walked toward the rushing sound of the waterfall.

"You needed a break. I wanted to take you somewhere where we could be ourselves, we didn't have to worry about pretending or cell phones or work."

"This is perfect."

Jenna's foot caught on a thick root, sending her tumbling against Mac. He caught her with his firm grip and held her tight. With her face right against his chest, she inhaled that familiar woodsy cologne and tried not to moan or close her eyes at the fact that just the smell of him turned her on. That's not what they were here for. He may have taken his flirty advances into another territory, but then he'd backed off. He'd wised up or given up, one of the two, and pushed her away.

So, whatever chance she may have had with her best friend, it was gone, and if she wanted to salvage the greatest friendship she'd ever had, she needed to cool it.

"Okay?" he asked, tipping her chin up.

With a nod, Jenna eased away. "I'm good. Just need to watch where I step."

He kept his hand in hers as he led her around the island. They discussed plants, flowers and he actually told her a few things she didn't know. Apparently the mysterious Mac O'Shea had done some homework before taking her out on this little excursion.

When he bent down to pluck a bright yellow flower, she halted her steps. He slid the blossom behind her ear, shoving her hair away, smoothing it on down past her shoulders. A shiver crept over her at the slightest touch and the way he seemed to be seducing her without even trying. Was he even aware of the effect he had on her?

"Don't look at me like that," he murmured, his fingertips trailing along her jawline before tapering off.

Jenna blinked and started walking ahead. Any response would only add fuel to the desire or start an argument, and at this point, they couldn't afford either.

The sound of the rushing water seemed to echo. Jenna walked on a few more steps then froze. She was at ground level with nature's pool, watching as the cascades fell over the edge of the cliff. The crystal water seemed so inviting, so refreshing. She'd worked up a slight sweat walking around, but she didn't mind one bit.

Slipping free of her flip-flops, Jenna tiptoed down to the water's edge. The coolness washed over her feet. She reached to the modest hem of her dress, and held it up as she waded in just a bit further.

Behind her, she heard Mac stepping in, as well. "This is perfect," he stated.

Keeping her back to him, she stopped when the water reached her knees. "I could stay here forever."

Only the sounds of a random bird chirping and the rushing of the waterfall enveloped them. Besides the beauty of their surroundings, there was nothing here that demanded their time or attention. Mac, Jenna and their own private island were all that existed in this world.

Jenna glanced over her shoulder and nearly gasped. Mac had taken his shirt off, those tanned muscles glistening in the sunshine. His board shorts were wet as he stepped in even further.

"If you want to take your dress off, there's no one else here," he told her.

Swallowing, Jenna kept her grip on the material bunched in her hand. "No, I'm…"

Mac stood only a few feet away, but he eased closer. "It's just me, Jenna. Don't be embarrassed."

"I only have on a bra and panties."

Mac quirked a brow. "And how is that different from a swimsuit?"

"I don't like wearing a suit, either."

"I know." He took her hand and opened her fingers, releasing the material. "You're beautifully made, no matter what you think or what you've been told. I'm not pressuring you, but if you want to swim in this once-in-a-lifetime place, then do it. Don't let insecurities rob you of this moment."

Why did he have to be so right? Why did he have to get inside her head and drive out all of the doubts? She'd justified each and every insecurity and felt she had a right to them. But when Mac talked to her, when he used that voice of reason, she listened. If she let her low self-esteem run her life, she'd miss out on some amazing things.

Turning away, she gripped the hem of her dress and slid it up over her head. Using the material as a shield, she moved closer to the shore and gave it a toss. Pulling in a deep breath, she rounded back and froze.

Mac's intense gaze was on hers, his hand extended, inviting her to join him.

Just friends.

Every now and then that reminder crept back into her head.

But there was something very intimate about being in a remote location with your friend, wearing nothing but your underwear.

No matter what happened today, this would be a memory she'd keep forever.

Twelve

What the hell was he thinking, inviting her to take that dress off? He'd slept in a damn hammock last night to avoid temptation and here he was begging for it to be rubbed in his face.

Jenna was absolutely breathtaking in her simple pink bra and panty set. Women threw themselves at him, purposely wore the sexiest of lingerie to entice him, but nothing got his attention more than a self-conscious Jenna wearing cotton. She moved him...so much that he had no idea what label to put on his emotions.

But he'd turned her away for a reason and he needed to keep in mind that, after this week, they both would return to Miami and the life they were used to. As friends.

Between thoughts of her in bed last night and texting Ryker, Mac hadn't gotten much sleep. Ryker was still playing cat and mouse with Shane. Unfortunately, Braden was still MIA and Mac was starting to worry.

He was also growing concerned he'd have to make a decision about Shane in short order.

Not something he wanted to think about while holding Jenna's hand in a place that could rival paradise.

"I know I keep saying it, but this place is so amazing."

She slid her hand free of his and ran her fingertips through the water. She dunked down so the water just skimmed the tops of her shoulders and Mac knew she was trying to keep her body hidden from him. He wasn't going to say anything. He didn't want to call her out or make her even more embarrassed. All he wanted was for her to see herself the way he did, the way any man with breath in his lungs would see a voluptuous woman.

"We probably shouldn't stay long, though."

Mac shook his head and slid onto his back to float.

"In a place like this, time doesn't exist."

"You're right. But I almost feel guilty for leaving and just—"

"Enjoying yourself?" he asked, coming back up to face her. "Don't feel guilty. The flowers are coming along so don't even think about those. And as for Martin, if I keep seeing him staring at you, I can't guarantee I'll hold myself back again."

Jenna laughed. "Hold yourself back? You punched him."

Mac nodded. "In my head I did more. He's lucky."

A sadness slipped over her features as she glanced away. "I wish you wouldn't be so cavalier about violence. You're too good of a man for that."

Mac clenched his teeth. He wasn't a good man. Moments ago he was contemplating making a call to end a life. There was evil in his family, though Braden was doing his damnedest to move away from that aspect of their activities. If Mac had to make the call, he would do so without a shadow of a doubt. He didn't make mistakes and he sure as hell wouldn't jump into a decision like this without fully analyzing every possible angle.

"You're my priority here," he told her. "You called me to help, and this is me helping. I don't like how he looks at you, how he treated you. He doesn't even deserve to be here, but that's not my call. I will protect you from getting hurt again, though. That much I can and will control."

Jenna's eyes widened; she bit down on her lower lip before turning away and diving into the water. She disappeared for a moment and popped up closer to the waterfall. With her dark hair slicked back, she looked like some type of dream rising from the waters. She was glorious, she was perfection…and for now she was his. He would resist temptation and give her this day of relaxation, no matter the cost to his feelings.

But taking his eyes off of her was not even a possibility. She floated easily on her back, her face tipped up to the sun, her mouth curved in a subtle smile that took his breath away.

Splashing water up onto his bare shoulders didn't help cool him off. Mac wasn't too certain anything would at this point. The sound of the rushing waterfall seemed to drown out everything else. Well, everything but his thoughts.

"You're frowning," Jenna stated as she waded closer to him. "How can anyone frown in a place like this?"

He blinked, attempting to will his demons away. "I didn't mean to."

As she neared him, her body lifted from the water as she threw her arms out to the side and closed her eyes. "I never want to leave. Ever."

He laughed at her childlike declaration, but as soon as she dropped her arms, the straps on her bra slid down over her shoulders. Without thinking, Mac reached out with both hands and pushed them back up. But instead of letting go and backing away, he curled his fingers around her wet, bare skin.

Those expressive eyes widened as she licked her bottom lip. Her heavy inhale pressed her chest out just enough to brush against his.

"Mac," she murmured.

"I know." Keeping his grip on her, he closed his eyes and told himself to pull away, but he couldn't. Not yet. "I didn't bring you here for this. But damn it, Jenna. I can't keep my hands off you."

With a tip of her chin, she reached up and held on to his wrists. "You know I won't be like all those other women in your life. That's not who I am."

Mac swallowed. "It's not who I want to be," he whispered. He had no idea if she heard him over the waterfall, but sleeping around wasn't something he'd set out to do. He'd never wanted a relationship, and being with women who were on the same page as him seemed to work. But right now, he felt...dirty. As if he wasn't good enough for her. He hated feeling like this.

Maybe he couldn't sleep with her, but that didn't mean he couldn't show her how much she meant to him.

With careful movements, and keeping his eyes on hers, he pushed the straps back down. Her hands remained around his wrists, but she didn't try to stop him. When he slid his fingertips over the flesh just above the lace trim of her bra, her body trembled beneath his touch.

When her hands tightened and she started to shake her head, Mac cut her off. "This isn't about me," he explained. "Let me show you."

Jenna remained silent, but held his gaze.

"Trust me," he added.

The slightest of nods gave him the green light he'd been waiting for. He hadn't even realized how monumental this was, but there was no way he could ever let her think she'd be like any other woman in his life. She was so much more.

She let go of his wrists, giving him complete control. Mac reached around and unfastened her bra, then removed the unwanted garment. Giving it a fling toward the shore, he allowed his eyes to rake over her exposed body. The water lapped just beneath her bare breasts and he could tell by the way she'd curled her body in and glanced away that she was vulnerable and doubting herself.

"You're the most beautiful woman, Jenna. Look at me," he commanded when she kept her eyes averted. "These perfect curves were made for a man's hands." *My hands.*

She didn't reply and he knew she didn't believe him. He was all too happy to show her exactly what he meant. Society had some warped idea of what a beautiful woman should look like, but in his opinion, a woman should be built like a woman. All curves and dips. A perfect layout to explore and enjoy.

Keeping his eyes locked on to hers, he wanted her to see every single emotion in his eyes. He wanted her to understand just how pivotal this moment was. And if he delved any more into that line of thinking, he'd terrify himself. But the last thing he wanted now was to pull away.

Mac cupped her face in his hands. "Don't take your eyes off me."

She didn't nod, didn't speak. She made no motion whatsoever. If Mac let his ego have control he'd think she was under his spell, but it was quite the opposite.

He cupped her breasts, loving how she quivered beneath his touch. When he moved his hands down her sides, she attempted to shift away.

"Never pull away from my touch."

Jenna froze. Keeping his eyes on hers, he let his palms travel over her soft skin beneath the water. Her stomach clenched, her hips tilted and he knew her body was reacting all on its own. Hooking his thumbs under the edge of her panties, he started pulling them down. A bit harder to do in the water, but he was a man with one goal in mind—to make Jenna feel like the beautiful, desirable woman she was.

"Brace your hands on my shoulders."

"Mac—"

"Do it."

Water trickled from her fingertips as she brought her hands from the water and placed them on his shoulders. Without another word, she lifted one foot at a time and let him remove the last of her clothing. Keeping one hand on her hip and the other between her thighs, he watched as her lids lowered halfway, desire completely consuming her. Her lips parted, a soft sigh escaped and Mac wanted more. Much more.

He wanted his name on her lips, he wanted her to know who was pleasuring her and why. He wanted Jenna to see this as much more than a quick release.

When he slid one finger over her center, her fingertips curled into his skin. Mac was barely hanging on by a thread because he couldn't wait to see her come undone. But Jenna was worth the wait.

As he moved his hand, she rocked her hips, never taking her eyes off him. There was something so intimate, so primal about watching her. He didn't think this much with other women, didn't analyze every detail. But he didn't want to mess up a single thing with Jenna.

Mac gripped her waist as his hand moved faster. Her body kept up with his rhythm and Mac watched as a pink tint crept over her face. A sheen of sweat covered her forehead and nose, but she never once took her eyes off him.

Her body jerked. "Mac, I'm—"

"Do it," he demanded.

When she tightened around him, his name slid off her lips like a whispered promise. Her eyes widened as if she wasn't expecting the onslaught. Mac held her close and kept pleasuring her until her body went lax.

Wrapping both hands around her waist, he pulled her against his chest. Her heartbeat seemed to be just as frantic as his own.

The sound of the rushing water, the occasional bird chirping and Jenna's panting were all music to his ears. Nothing else mattered but this moment, this woman. Words eluded him. Honestly, if he opened his mouth right now, he didn't know what he'd say. He was aching to be with her, but he wouldn't put her in that position. Beyond that, he wanted to say something sweet, something romantic…but that wasn't them. They weren't here for romance and he sure as hell didn't want her to get the wrong idea.

Jenna's hand slid over his board shorts, heading toward the one spot he needed her most. But he pulled away.

"No."

Jerking back, her brows drew in as she searched his face. "Why?"

Mac clenched his teeth. "This isn't about me or even us. This was all for you."

A slight grin tipped one corner of her mouth. "Hardly seems fair."

Taking her hands in his, he kissed her fingertips and placed her palms flat on his chest. "I don't want you to think you're like other women. This wasn't about sex, Jenna. I need you to know that."

She stared at him for a moment without saying a word. "I don't know what to think," she finally said. "You don't want anything in return?"

With a painful laugh, Mac shook his head. "You already know the answer to that, but you deserve more and I never want you to think that you're in a group with any other woman I've been with. You're completely different. I've never…"

Damn it. He didn't plan on confessing his doubts. He wanted to pleasure her, enjoy a little swim, have a few laughs and fly back to their bungalow. Why did this have to be so difficult?

"You've never what?" she prompted, moving closer to wrap her arms around his neck.

Swallowing any fear of opening up to her, Mac stated, "I've never just given without expecting something in return. I've never wanted to. A relationship has never been in the future for me so I always make sure to…"

Mercy. The more his thoughts started taking a stroll out of his mouth, the more he sounded like a jerk.

"I've been a bastard," he confessed, guilt slamming into his chest and squeezing like a vice. "I purposely find women who only want one thing and then I move on. I never set out to be that way, Jenna, and I don't know why I'm telling you this."

Mac dropped his head because the last thing he wanted was for Jenna to see him vulnerable or broken. Damn it, he hadn't even known how much this hurt him until he started saying the words out loud. He'd used his body in an attempt to ignore all the anxiety and fear that came with relationships. And maybe he hadn't even noticed until right now.

"You're telling me because you care." She tipped his chin up and he was rewarded with a megawatt smile that told him she completely understood and wasn't judging. "You're telling me because you value our friendship and you don't want to hurt me. And I never thought you were a bastard."

Mac reached up and framed her face. With her lush wet body plastered against his, he never wanted to leave this place, either. Why couldn't they just run away and be—

Wait. What the hell was he thinking? Run away? As in, together? He didn't have time or the emotional stability to attempt anything like a relationship and he sure as hell wouldn't make Jenna his guinea pig.

Just because he'd had some grand epiphany over his suppressed emotions like some damn woman didn't mean he wanted to explore boyfriend territory. He was still out for a good time…he just wanted that with Jenna and then he wanted to move on.

Damn it. He'd created a giant mess and plopped her right smack dab in the middle.

"What you did just now." She bit down on her lip before continuing. "Nobody has ever put my needs first. The way you look at me, the way you touch me…"

"What?" He wanted to hear her say it. Needed to hear her say it. And that made him not only a bastard, but a masochist, because he had nothing to offer her beyond the physical.

"You make me feel beautiful," she whispered.

Every part of Mac wanted to rejoice in the fact that

she'd finally seen herself as he did. "You are, Jenna. I've been trying to tell you that, and I needed to show you. It's been hell trying to keep my hands off you, but I didn't know another way. I wanted you to see how desirable you are, how much a man can completely break by being near you. You've got this power I don't even think you are aware of possessing."

Toying with the ends of his wet hair, Jenna held his gaze. "Things won't be weird between us, will they? Because I can't lose you."

"No," he vowed, praying he wasn't lying. "You won't lose me."

But he wouldn't, couldn't ignore this ache. No matter the internal battle he'd been waging with himself, Mac had gotten the briefest glimpse of Jenna's passion. He knew there was so much more to uncover and he planned on doing just that in the remaining days. He could figure out what to do for the long term later.

First things first. Jenna would be his.

Thirteen

The ride back in the helicopter was…strained. So much for things not getting weird. Of course, she couldn't even think about the tension that had settled between them because her body was still humming from that entire experience in the pool by the waterfall.

Oh, mercy, her best friend had skills. Why? Why did they have to be so compatible in the sexual department, too? Why did every part of her still ache for more, even after he'd satisfied her?

What did they talk about now? Seriously. Because no matter what subject they broached, she wasn't sure she could give up any of her mind space to mundane things.

So, silence it was, since he was apparently not up for a chat, either. Was he having regrets?

No. That was one thing she was pretty certain of. He'd made it a point to tell her she was different from other women. His raw honesty had surprised her. She'd never gotten a sense of any vulnerability from him whatsoever. He'd always been so strong, so confident…so many things she wasn't.

But maybe they were more alike than she'd ever thought.

Once they were back on the main island, they walked to their bungalow. Silence still accompanied them and she worried just how they'd finish out these last few days.

As they headed down the dock toward their hut, Jenna slowed. "My sister and my mom—"

"I see them," he said, reaching for her hand and giving it a slight squeeze.

A sense of relief speared her. She didn't even know she'd been holding her breath, but with the simplest of touches, some of the tension left her in a long exhale.

Then she remembered the charade. He'd most likely taken her hand because her family was watching. That had to be it, because he'd not touched her and barely spoken a word since…the moment she didn't even have a name for.

"There you guys are," her mother exclaimed. "We just knocked and wondered where you went."

Jenna pasted on a smile, a bit relieved that others were here as a buffer. How ridiculous was that? Since when did she need a buffer between her and her best friend? This entire situation had gotten out of control and if she didn't do something to reverse this mess, she'd risk losing the best thing that had ever happened to her.

"I hope we can steal your woman away for a few hours," her mother went on, oblivious to the turmoil.

Mac stiffened at her side, she had to assume over the whole "your woman" comment. Jenna tried not to take it personally, though it was rather difficult. Everything about this week, this farce, had become personal.

"We thought with the rehearsal tomorrow and the wedding the next day, we'd take you out tonight." Amy beamed and clasped her hands. "Just us girls."

The thought of going into that bungalow alone with Mac, who may or may not be regretting what they'd just done, didn't exactly appeal to her. She may be a coward, but she needed time to think. Time away from his intense stare, time from his kisses, his touches…

"Give me a few minutes to wash up," she told them, pulling her hand from Mac's. "We found the most incredible waterfall and—"

Oh, no. Was she really going to start in on why she needed a quick shower? Her hair was clearly damp, her clothes were clinging to the wet parts of her body. It was obvious she hadn't just been out on a stroll.

"Go right ahead." Jenna's mom turned her smile toward Mac. "We'll keep him company. I want to hear all about what you've done today."

That's precisely what she was afraid of and why she had to get ready in record time.

"Make the call."

Mac sank down onto the leather sofa in the bungalow, rubbed his forehead and gripped his cell. Ryker's demand was simple, yet so difficult to act on.

"Shane isn't backing down," Ryker went on. "He actually intercepted a piece of art that's due for your auction in Miami in two weeks. It was a legitimate piece, not one we had to acquire, but he's showing his hand."

Which meant the O'Sheas needed to show theirs. Shane was ballsy, that was for damn sure. The man obviously didn't know who he was dealing with, or he was too stupid to care.

But to make the ultimate call on a death was not something Mac took lightly. Still, Shane had threatened Laney and now he was throwing his weight around like he could control the O'Shea family. Hell, no. That man had been a proverbial thorn in their side for years and the fact he thought he could use power against them was unacceptable. But trying to kidnap their sister was grounds for the ultimate punishment.

"I left a voicemail for Braden, but he hasn't returned my call."

Which meant the decision was Mac's to make. Obviously Ryker's choice was to end the conflict before it caused even more trouble. But Mac was starting to get even more concerned with Braden's silence. This wasn't like him and if Mac hadn't been so wrapped up in Jenna, he would've focused more on his own family than his hormones.

"Let me try to reach Braden one more time," Mac said. "I'll let you know."

"Make it fast. I'm done with this guy."

Mac hung up and eased forward, placing his elbows on his knees. Nothing kept Braden quiet for this long. Something was wrong and Mac couldn't tackle any other issue until he knew what it was.

He called Braden, not surprised when he got voicemail, too. After leaving an urgent message, Mac fired off a text. Maybe if he kept badgering him, Braden would answer.

Pushing off the couch, Mac stalked to the fridge to grab a bottle of water. Of course, he had to be careful of the blooms in there because Jenna would murder him in his sleep if he so much as touched a petal.

After grabbing a water, really wishing he had something stronger, he took his phone and the bottle to the deck. His mind was a jumbled mess, between the Shane situation, his brother's unexplained absence and the encounter with Jenna at the waterfall.

Standing on the edge of the deck, watching the orange sun settle on the horizon, Mac recalled the way Jenna had responded so perfectly to his touch. All that pent-up passion just waiting for the right man to come along and release it. For reasons he didn't even want to explain to himself, he wanted to be that man. He wanted nothing more than to...

What? He wanted her in his bed and beyond that he couldn't make plans. He'd be heading back to Miami as soon as this wedding was over because he had an auction that would be in the final stretch of preparations.

Mac took a long pull of his water and willed his phone to vibrate. After waiting another ten minutes, he shot off another text, demanding a reply of any kind or he'd be on the next flight to Boston.

After a few minutes, Braden's reply came.

Zara and I are dealing with something. Don't come home, but business is on you for the next few days. Will talk in person later.

Well, that answered one question but stirred up a whole host of others. What was going on with Braden and Zara? Surely not relationship issues. Those two were so in love it was almost sickening. Braden was so protective, so fierce about keeping Zara safe from their world. Surely nothing had happened to Zara. If so, Braden would've called in all forces to deal with the issue.

Then what was going on?

Mac finished off his water and sighed. At least Braden was safe, but the fact he'd passed all business decisions to Mac spoke volumes as to the severity of Braden's problem.

This also meant Mac would have to make a decision about Ryker's pressing matter.

Damn it.

Mac knew Braden wanted this family to take a less aggressive role in battling their enemies, but Shane had proven time and again that he was nothing more than a menace. He harassed Zara, he'd fought with their late father more than once and now he was getting too close to their main goal of retrieving the scrolls. Mac had to assume that's why he intercepted the recent art, just to prove he could get that close to their operation and slip beneath their noses unnoticed.

Unacceptable.

But, trying to take Laney was an act that could not be overlooked. The man was dead.

Gripping his empty bottle in one hand, Mac shot off a text to Ryker.

Finish it. Text me when you're done.

And with that weighty decision made, he went inside in search of something stronger than water.

Jenna walked back to her bungalow after an amazing dinner and laughs with her mom and sister, still anxious about being alone with Mac. They'd both had time to reevaluate everything and perhaps they could just ignore the fact that he'd given her the most intense sexual experience of her life. Well, maybe *he* could, but she wasn't so sure.

What would happen when she walked in that door? It was late, nearing midnight. Maybe he'd be asleep.

Jenna, Amy and their mom had eaten, gone for dessert, then ended up at their mother's bungalow where they'd discussed memories, good and bad, chatted weddings and even shed a few tears over the monumental day fast approaching.

Now here she was afraid to open the door to her own hut because she had no clue what waited on the other side.

Pulling in a deep breath, she adjusted her strapless sundress, gripped her purse and pushed the door open. Darkness greeted her, along with a sliver of disappointment. Part of her had wanted Mac to be waiting up for her. Going to bed with this sexual tension surrounding them would only cause another sleepless night.

"I didn't think you were coming back."

Jenna jumped and glanced toward the bedroom, where Mac's outline filled the doorway. His arms were braced on the frame above his head, and in the darkness the moonlight cast a soft glow into the hut, showcasing the perfection of his chiseled arms, his broad, bare chest and his narrow waist.

Jenna swallowed and dropped her clutch on the accent table beside the door. "We lost track of time. What did you do while I was gone?"

There. Keep the conversation friendly.

But when Mac pushed off the door and stalked toward her in that sexy, panther-like way, she had a feeling the friendly talk was finished.

"I don't want to talk about what I did." His growl washed over her body, sending shivers and goose bumps racing across her skin. "I don't want to talk at all."

"Mac—"

"No." With the gap closed between them, he placed his hands on either side of her head, caging her against the door. "We've danced around this attraction long enough. After today, I can't ignore it anymore."

Jenna licked her lips, aching with the desire to touch him, to be touched by him. "And what about tomorrow? Or when we get back to Miami?"

"We'll worry about it then."

His lips crushed hers as he gripped her dress and yanked it down, leaving the material to pool at her feet.

Well, that answered one question. She knew what to expect tonight and she wasn't about to put a stop to it, no matter what red flags were waving in her mind. For once, she was going to do what she wanted, damn the consequences.

Mac couldn't touch her enough. Between their excitement at the waterfall earlier and the business decision he'd had to make, Mac was strung way too tight. He needed Jenna, needed to feel her desire, her passion.

She pressed her lush body against his as he continued kissing her. Delicate hands gripped his shoulders. The bite of her nails into his skin only added to the pleasure.

Reaching behind her back, he unfastened her strapless bra and flung it to the side. Hooking his thumbs into her panties, he jerked those down, too. He wanted her completely naked, completely his.

"Mac." She pulled away, panting.

He trailed his lips down her throat and palmed her breasts in his hands. "I have to have you, Jenna."

She cupped the side of his face, pulling his attention up toward her heavy-lidded eyes. "Then have me."

Mac took her hands and put them on the waistband of his shorts. "Show me you want this."

Without hesitation, she removed his shorts, leaving him just as bare as she was. "I can't go slow," he warned. "I want you too much."

"I won't break, Mac. Do what you want."

Like a dam that had burst, he captured her lips once again. With one hand firmly gripping her waist, Mac slid his other hand between her legs. As she stepped apart, he touched her just enough to have her moaning into the kiss.

When he said he couldn't wait, he hadn't been lying. For days he'd been hanging on by a thread and today that thread finally snapped. He broke the kiss, reached down to his shorts and snagged the condom from the pocket.

"Looks like you planned this," she murmured, her chest heaving.

"I'm not sorry."

After covering himself, he stepped back against her and grabbed hold of her hips. "Wrap your legs around my waist."

"I'm too heavy," she argued, her eyes darting away.

"Do it," he commanded. "And never look away from me again."

The second her legs were wrapped around him, Mac slid into her. For a second, he didn't move, couldn't move. She was utterly, blissfully perfect, wrapped all around him in every way possible. Jenna held her breath; her eyes widened but remained on his.

He had no clue what emotions were lurking in his own eyes and he damn well didn't want to get into analyzing them, especially when Jenna's curves were all his for the taking.

Her hips started moving as her body arched. Those pants and moans of hers were killing him. Finally, she was letting go of that control she clung so tightly to.

And Mac finally did what he'd been dying to do for years. He ran his hands all over the luscious dips and valleys of her bare body. Each time he brushed the sides of her breasts, Jenna let out another moan.

When he feasted on them, she cried out his name.

Her body tightened, her fingertips curled deeper into his shoulders as her release swept over her. Mac pulled back, needing to see her face, wanting to watch as she came apart.

And he wasn't disappointed. Her eyes were locked on his, just as he'd demanded. A sheen of perspiration covered the bridge of her nose as she opened her mouth and cried out.

Mac couldn't hold back another second. He pumped harder, tumbling over the edge and clinging to Jenna as if she was his lifeline, as if she was every single thing he'd been waiting for his whole life.

His state of euphoria was overwhelming. Never before had so many emotions swept through him at once, and every single thing he was feeling was all because of Jenna.

And even though he'd told her to keep her eyes on him, he had to close his. He couldn't afford for her to see everything he was feeling…not when he wasn't ready to face the truth himself.

Fourteen

Mac lay in bed beside Jenna and watched her sleep. He couldn't shut his mind down even if he wanted to. After their intense encounter against the front door, Mac had carried her to bed where she'd promptly drifted off to sleep. Yet even in her sleep she kept a hand on him.

Swallowing his guilt, Mac stared at her delicate fingers on his abdomen. She'd given herself so completely, so honestly, and he wasn't worthy of any of it. He'd planned on taking her tonight. Had planned on making her his, when the last thing he deserved was sweet Jenna in his life, let alone his bed.

He'd ordered a kill only hours earlier and the reality still weighed heavily on his shoulders. He'd made the call in the past, but that was when his father had been alive and the situation called for such extremes.

Now his father was gone, Braden was incapacitated and Mac was in charge. Ryker had demanded over and over that Mac let him do his job and Mac knew Ryker didn't kill just for sport. The man may be their secret weapon, but he was also a professional. If there was another way, Ryker would've found it.

Still, Mac had made the final decision.

Delaying any longer could result in Laney getting hurt, even killed. Braden, Mac and Ryker preferred to keep Laney on the technical side of the family business and not in harm's way. But Shane was a ticking time bomb. Who's to say he wouldn't come for Zara—or even Jenna? The man was smart enough to know who mattered most in the lives of the men he was trying so hard to bring down.

Shane had to be stopped, permanently. Braden would understand.

Mac laid his hand over Jenna's as if to draw some of her innocence into his life. She was sweet, charmingly so, and completely the opposite of what his world entailed.

She arranged flowers for a living, for crying out loud. She literally made things around her beautiful while he dealt with lying, stealing…and murder.

His chest ached because no matter what he wanted, anything beyond a physical connection was impossible. But he hadn't been able to hold himself back any longer. Jenna had stirred something in him so primal, he needed her like nothing he'd ever known. And that fact scared the hell out of him.

Jenna shifted in her sleep and rolled toward him. Mac lifted his arm, allowing her to nestle deeper into his side. Call him a bastard, but he wasn't about to push her away. No, he didn't deserve her, but he wanted her. He was an O'Shea. They saw something they wanted and they took it. Simple as that.

For tonight, Jenna was his. She trusted him with her body and she'd given him full control. Only days ago they'd been friends pretending to be more. Could Jenna slip back into the friend role once this wedding was over?

The bigger question was, could he?

Jenna stood back and stared at the flower arrangements in the dining area where the reception would be held tomorrow. Everything was absolutely perfect. The purple from the lavender popped against the white tablecloths and the greenery. The fresh, yet simple arrangements were just what Amy had asked for.

The room was breathtaking anyway, with floor-to-ceiling windows encompassing the entire back wall. With the ocean view and the romantic ambiance inside, the small reception tomorrow would be absolutely stunning.

"Looks beautiful."

Jenna spun around to see Martin standing in the doorway. Great. The last person she wanted to be alone with.

Mac had gone back to the bungalow after he'd helped her carry the arrangements in. He'd stated he had some work to finish up, but she had the feeling something was bothering him so she let him go without question. After the sex they'd had, she was more confused than ever and perhaps he was, too.

"I'm not in the mood right now, Martin."

She had been given the okay to stay in the event space as late as she needed as long as she found a worker to lock up when she was done. This way no one would bother her…well, no one was supposed to bother her.

"I didn't come to argue," Martin told her. "I actually came to tell you that even though I think you're making a mistake, I'm not going to pursue you—us—any longer."

Jenna crossed her arms, not bothering to comment on the fact there was no "us" where she and Martin were concerned.

"What changed your mind?" she asked, her attention fixed on his bruised eye, compliments of Mac.

"Whatever you and O'Shea have going on is something beyond what you and I had." Martin shrugged and shoved his hands in the pockets of his shorts. "I saw how he looked at you during the rehearsal. He stayed on the sidelines, but his eyes never left you. He's intense, and I'm not getting in the way of what you have."

Jenna figured he didn't want to get in the way of Mac, period, but she kept her opinion to herself.

Had Mac been focused on her the entire time? She'd glanced his way more than once during the rehearsal and had seen him looking her way, but…the entire time? Maybe last night had switched something in him. Perhaps he was looking at her as more than every other woman who came before her. Maybe he'd been telling the truth when he told her she was special.

Jenna focused on Martin, still standing only a few feet away. "I'm glad you're moving on," she told him.

Martin nodded, then stared at her another minute as if he wanted to say something else, but finally he turned and walked away. Jenna blew out a breath and turned to survey the room one last time.

The lights went off and before she could fully react, a reflection in the windows caught her attention. Barely had she spun around when hands curled over her shoulders, lips feasted on the delicate spot beneath her ear.

"Stubborn man finally came to his senses," Mac growled. "And now you're done and all alone."

The veiled promise had Jenna shivering. "I thought you had work."

"I did."

He snaked an arm around her waist and drew her body

back against his. Her head fell against his shoulder as his lips continued to slide up and down her heated skin.

"You know what I've thought about all day?" he muttered against her neck.

"Wh-what?"

"Seeing if we can make last night's encounter seem tame."

Jenna gasped as Mac whirled her around in his arms, her body crushed against his as he slammed his mouth onto hers. Wrapping her arms around him, she opened, needing to feel that connection and anxiously wanting him to deliver on that promise.

"We can't do this here," she managed to mumble against his mouth.

"I locked the door after he left. Nothing to stop us."

Anticipation rolled through her as she threaded her fingers through his hair and tugged. "Then you better get to work because last night was pretty amazing."

His lips tilted into a grin. "Is that a dare?"

"Take it how you want."

"I'd rather take you how I want."

Mac smacked her bottom and grabbed hold of her as he walked her backward toward the dark corner away from the windows. She didn't want to analyze what it meant that he'd come to her and was so eager to have her. She only wanted Mac, wanted this experience that was unlike any other.

He kissed her lips, her neck, her bare shoulders. He eased the thin straps of her dress down, tugging until the scoop neckline fell below her breasts.

"You're so damn sexy, Jenna."

Pretty words could be said by anyone, but the way Mac showed her how he felt had Jenna believing every word. He did find her sexy, and because of that she had a confidence she'd never known before.

Feeling daring, she whispered, "Then stop talking and show me."

Mac sat her on the edge of a built-in bar and stepped between her spread legs. He grabbed a condom from his pocket, ever prepared, and rid himself of his shorts. Laying the foil packet beside her hip, he quirked a brow.

"You have on too many clothes."

Whipping the dress up and over her head, she tossed it to the floor. Were they really going to do this here? In the wide open room where anyone with the key could walk in and flip on the light?

Jenna had never thought herself staid, but this wasn't something she'd ever even imagined. Somehow sex always conjured up images of a bed, yet she and Mac had never even considered getting between the sheets.

After she wrestled out of her panties, Mac grabbed her hand and placed the condom in her palm. The silent command sent an even bigger charge of arousal shooting through her. She ripped open the packet and carefully covered him. She'd never done that with a lover before.

Mac cupped the back of her head with one hand and placed the other one on the small of her back, pulling her to the edge of the bar. Jenna slid her knees up his sides and locked her ankles behind him as he surged into her.

"Lean back."

Following his orders, she eased back slightly on her hand and watched as he took total control. With only the moonlight streaming in through the windows behind him, she had a sense of deja vu from the previous night. But this was better, far better. The nerves were gone, replaced by passion and need.

The desire that coiled low in her belly spread warmth

throughout her body as Mac gripped her hips and kept his eyes locked on to hers. She didn't know how he managed to make her feel so special and, dare she say, loved. She knew this wasn't love, not in the sense she'd like, but he cared for her, he wanted to be with her and she'd have to be content with the here and now.

Jenna tipped her head back, bowing her body when the pleasure became too much. Mac reached between them, touching her in the most intimate spot, sending Jenna spiraling out of control.

Bright light burst behind her lids as her entire body convulsed. Mac's body stilled against hers as he leaned forward and covered her mouth with his. She wrapped her arms around him as they tumbled into the abyss together.

Heavy breathing filled the silence of the room as reality settled back in. What would happen next? Would they go back to the bungalow and sleep together as they had done last night? Would she wake up in his arms again?

With the wedding tomorrow, she wondered just how far Mac intended to take this escapade. Only time would tell, but Jenna had another day to enjoy her best friend and she intended to do just that.

Fifteen

Mac watched as Jenna hugged the bride. The ceremony had been beautiful, if weddings were your thing. They were definitely not Mac's, but keeping his eyes on Jenna in her pale purple, figure-hugging dress was.

He didn't know how much longer he could handle being this close to Jenna and not touching her. And, lucky for Martin, he'd managed to keep his eyes averted for the most part.

Jenna crossed the outdoor seating area that had been set up specifically for this event. Even the way she glided through the white chairs had Mac's gut clenching. Everything about Jenna was getting to him. Her touch, her glances, the smile she'd thrown his way during the ceremony. No other woman had ever gotten beneath his skin and made him want more.

"Are you ready to escort me to the reception?" she asked as she neared.

Mac hooked his arm out and offered her a smile. "I don't think we'll be able to enjoy that room as much as we did last night."

She looped her arm through his and laughed. "No, I don't think we will."

Because he couldn't resist, Mac leaned down and whispered, "I plan on stripping you out of that dress when we get back and showing you exactly how sexy you looked today."

When her body trembled against his, Mac eased back and smiled. "Shall we?"

She turned her attention toward the rest of the wedding party filing into the dining area. "I may need a minute after that."

"Don't take too long or everyone is going to see just how hot I am for you."

"Come on," she stated, tugging him toward the open doors. "A toast, the cake and then we're out of here."

Mac laughed at her eager tone. They couldn't get out of this place fast enough. For once he wanted her in a bed, he wanted slow and he wanted to explore her the way she deserved.

Another first. He'd never once wanted to take his time. With every other woman he'd been there for one reason: release. With Jenna...he blew out a sigh. With Jenna, his life was completely different and he still had no idea how he was going to manage to let her go tomorrow.

But holding on to her would only prove to be a disaster in the long run. She didn't do secrets and lies. She didn't do dark and deceptive. Jenna was literally sunshine and flowers and happiness.

He may be a jerk for stealing some of her sweetness, but he had never been able to resist temptation and Jenna LeBlanc was temptation personified.

As they entered the bright room with the sun bursting through the wall of windows, he watched Jenna's eyes dart to the bar in the corner.

"Keep that in mind for later," he whispered.

He attempted to ignore the mental image of the two of them on that bar last night, but the force was too strong and the experience too fierce. Jenna had opened up so much over the past two days. Just the thought of exploring every inch of her when they returned to the bungalow was almost like foreplay.

"The place looks gorgeous."

Mac turned to see Mary smiling from ear to ear. Jenna released her hold on Mac and hugged her mother.

"It's a perfect day, isn't it?" Jenna asked.

Mac heard that wistfulness in her voice and wondered if she was thinking ahead to her own wedding...to some faceless bastard Mac already hated. But Jenna would, in fact, move on and she would marry because the whole family life was what she wanted. Who was he to prevent her from being happy and going after her dream with both hands?

That didn't mean he had to like it.

Mac excused himself as the two ladies chatted about the spectacular ceremony. He needed a drink. He'd prefer to hit something, but a drink would have to do, considering his location. When he returned to Miami, he and his punching bag were going to have some serious bonding time.

The bartender hooked Mac up with his favorite bourbon. Leaning one elbow on the edge of the bar, Mac swirled the amber liquid around and watched as the bride and groom came together in the middle of the floor for their first dance. That wasn't all he noticed. The soft, dreamy look in Jenna's eyes as she watched the couple was like a punch to Mac's gut.

Did she even know how radiant she was? How magnificent she looked when she was daydreaming? And there wasn't a doubt in his mind that the thoughts running through her head hinged on this beautiful day.

He watched her for the rest of the dance. But, when the music changed he couldn't wait another second. Without taking his eyes off her, Mac placed his glass on the bar and crossed the room. Her eyes met his, a ghost of a smile flirted around those kissable lips. He said nothing as he took her in his arms and started swaying to the subtle beat.

Her floral scent surrounded him, her delicate arms circled his waist as she laid her head on his chest. Why did holding her so intimately have his heart clenching? Everything in his life to this point had been simple regarding women. He saw what he wanted, he took it, he walked away.

But leaving Jenna seemed so cold, so harsh. And he wasn't referring to the physical leaving, but the mental form. Spending this week with Jenna had been…refreshing. He hadn't expected to be so relaxed in some ways and so worked up in others. This one woman managed to do what so many others had tried. She'd gotten under his skin and he didn't know what the hell to do.

Well, he knew what he wanted to do.

Mac's hands spread across her bare back, just above where the material draped low. He'd seen a confidence in her this week, almost a blossoming. She'd been so worried about her body, her very lush, sexy body, but he'd proven to her that she was built like every man's dream.

His dream.

Damn it. He didn't want to have a dream woman. There was no such thing in his world.

Mac closed his eyes and pushed every doubt and worry aside. For these next few moments, he just wanted to enjoy the feel of Jenna in his arms.

As the song ended, Jenna eased back and glanced up at him with desire burning in her eyes. Without a word, she took his hand and he gladly let her lead him out of the reception, out into the evening and toward their bungalow.

He fished the key from his pocket and unlocked the door. Jenna pulled him inside and when the door closed at his back, she turned and caged him in. With her body flush against his and her hands framing his face, she pulled him down and captured his lips.

Never in his life had an aggressive woman turned him on so much. He'd always thrived on control, on being in charge in his work and in the bedroom. But Jenna had fully come out of her shell and damn if he wasn't proud.

Mac gripped her waist, jerking her hips forcefully against his. As much as he wanted this fast and hard, he craved something different, something more. Jenna deserved more. Hadn't he said that all along?

While he couldn't give her a commitment, he could give her tonight. He wanted her to remember this, remember him…forever?

Forever wasn't a word he used.

Focusing on Jenna, Mac slid his hands up her bare back and reached for the thick straps on her shoulders. As he eased them aside, she frantically pushed her dress down and stepped back. The material pooled around her feet, leaving her in a strapless white bra and killer pair of panties.

Even though Mac intended to take things slow tonight, he wasn't about to stop her when she reached around and unhooked her bra. Only a few days ago she never would've done this in front of him. His heart quickened as she flung the garment aside and worked the lacy white panties down her shapely legs.

Jenna reached up, pulled a few pins from her hair and Mac's knees nearly buckled when that hair came tumbling down over her bare shoulders. He couldn't recall a more beautiful sight.

Cocking her head to the side, she quirked a brow. "Your move."

Damn, she was something else.

"What if I want to stand here and stare at you a bit longer?" he asked.

He heard her breath catch in her throat, watched as her eyes widened and her mouth froze in a perfect O.

Mac pushed off the door and, in one swift move, lifted her in his arms with one hand behind her back and the other beneath her knees.

"You can't—"

"I can," he stated, cutting off her protest. "And I am. I want you on the bed, our bed. All night."

She trembled against him as she laced her fingers behind his neck. She wanted him to make a move? Then this was it. He was spending the next several hours making her his, making this last impression of their time in Bora Bora absolutely unforgettable.

With the door to the private deck open, the sheers billowed in, the moon slashed a glow directly across the bed. And that's where Mac laid her. He wanted her wearing nothing but moonlight.

He eased back and Jenna started to get up.

"Don't move," he commanded. "I'm going to look at you while I undress."

Slowly, she lay back down, her eyes locked on his.

While he made quick work of the buttons on his dress shirt, he smiled as her gaze dipped down to his body. Having Jenna's eyes on him gave him a rush like nothing else. For the first time in, well, ever, he wanted approval from a lover. He wanted approval from Jenna.

Mac gave his shirt a toss to the side of the room and shed his tux pants and boxer briefs. He took a step toward the bed and ran his fingertips over the curve of her knee and up her thigh. The silkiness of her skin beneath his hands—hands that had done terrible things in his world—was a reminder of how different they were. But for now, they weren't Mac the Mafia Mogul and Jenna the Sweet Florist. They were a man and a woman who enjoyed each other, who wanted the same thing for tonight and didn't care what tomorrow would bring.

There was no tomorrow as far as he was concerned. The world could end right now and Mac would die a happy man. Then he wouldn't have to walk away and—

"What do you think about when you're looking at me like that?" she asked, breaking into thoughts that had no place in his mind.

Sliding in beside her, Mac continued exploring her body. "I'm thinking how lucky I am that you asked me here this week." He trailed his fingertips over her hip, across her quivering stomach. "I'm thinking that touching you is the single most important thing in my life right now."

Jenna reached up, running her hand along his jawline. "What are we doing here, Mac?"

He swallowed. He didn't want these questions, the ones he couldn't answer, settling between them in the bed. All he wanted was Jenna. He wanted to show her how magnificent she was and that nothing should ever bring her back down again. Not weight, not self-esteem and sure as hell not a man.

"We're about to have a memorable night," he whispered as he dipped his head toward her breast and slid his hand over the dip in her waist. "We're about to ignore the outside world and pretend nothing else exists."

She threaded her fingers through his hair. The slight tug had Mac smiling against her damp skin.

"You with me, Jen?"

Arching up to meet his lips, she replied, "I'm with you. I never want to be anywhere else."

Mac ignored the stab of guilt, the sliver of fear he felt at her statement. They were getting caught up in the moment. She knew where he stood and grasped that this was their last night together.

Mac focused on pleasuring her, on keeping his name on her lips each time she moaned or cried out. When he hovered over her, Jenna's hands trailed up his biceps as she looked him in the eye.

"I want nothing between us tonight," she whispered. "I'm on birth control and I'm clean."

Mac had never, ever been without protection. That was a major no-no. Most of the women he'd been with he'd just met and they didn't stick around long enough to earn his trust. But with Jenna, he trusted her completely and when her legs wrapped around his waist he said nothing as he pushed forward.

Gripping the comforter for some shred of control, Mac shut his eyes and willed his body to stay still. He wanted to savor this moment, being with Jenna in every single way possible. With absolutely nothing between them, Mac pulled in a deep breath and started to move. Jenna had literally wrapped herself around him.

"Look at me." He always wanted her eyes on him,

but right now, this second, was most important. "Only me, Jenna."

She tightened all around him and cried out, "Only you."

As Mac's release slammed into him, he captured her mouth. He couldn't get close enough to her and he wanted to make this moment last. Jenna's nails bit into his shoulders as she trembled and finally, her body went lax beneath his.

Mac eased to the side, tucking her against him. When her hand settled over his heart, the irony was not lost on him. She'd stolen it. The one thing in this world he swore he'd never give had been taken by his best friend.

None of this was okay. He didn't want to give her his heart, he didn't want Jenna in his world in every way possible. How could he protect her from all the questionable dealings he encountered? He'd just ordered a man killed, for pity's sake, so she obviously needed protection from the filthy life he led.

He'd never hurt her, though. Not physically, not emotionally. He'd kill anyone if they laid a finger on her.

Heaviness washed over Mac as Jenna's breathing softened. He laid his hand over hers, wanting to savor the moment a bit longer, but the flashing light from his phone on the dresser told him business was calling. His time in fairy-tale land was over.

Sixteen

Jenna rolled over, stretched and smiled as memories washed over her. Last night had been amazing.

Squinting against the sunlight streaming through the sheers, Jenna reached across the bed…encountering cool sheets. She sat up and glanced around the bedroom. The empty bedroom.

As she surveyed the area, she thought Mac could be in the living room or making breakfast to surprise her in bed, but she knew better. He was gone. There wasn't a stitch of his clothing in here, no bag, no shoes. Absolutely nothing.

With the rumpled sheets and the masculine scent of Mac still all around, Jenna might as well be mocked for her error in judgment. She'd been afraid to get this close, to let her defenses down where Mac was concerned, but she'd taken a risk. She'd known the consequences going in and she'd said to hell with it.

Well, now she sat here all alone in a bed where they'd been intimate only hours ago, which just proved she'd been right all along. Nothing and no one could change Mac O'Shea.

Even knowing all of this, even having her eyes wide open to the inevitable ending, didn't stop the hurt from spearing directly into her heart. Last night when they'd made love—and that's exactly what they did—he'd looked into her eyes, he'd held her like a man who was falling. She'd thought for sure they were feeling the same thing.

What they shared was so much more than physical closeness. They'd had a deep bond long before their clothes fell off.

Sinking back against the pillows, throat tight and eyes burning, Jenna scolded herself. What would crying do? Mac would still be gone and she'd still be here looking like a complete and utter fool.

Part of her wished he'd taken off because he was afraid. At least then she'd know he'd seen her as something more than just a friend or a casual romp. Nothing about this entire week had been casual, but Mac was done here. He'd fulfilled his obligation, his friendly duties, and he was off.

Jenna clutched the sheet to her chest and rolled over, away from the scent of Mac's pillow. The pain intensified the longer she lay there, but she couldn't bring herself to get out of bed. She knew Mac left because he told her he would, and Mac always kept his word.

Where was he now? On a flight back to Barcelona or wherever he'd come from before riding to her rescue? Was he going to meet up with one of his ladies, resume his life as though it was business as usual?

Jenna wished like hell she could be that blasé about

sex, but she just couldn't. She'd grown up dreaming of finding the love of her life, of being with the man who made her heart flip in her chest. From the second she'd seen Mac at the party of a mutual friend, her heart hadn't stopped flipping.

But they had completely different ideas regarding relationships...namely that he didn't want one and she did.

Jenna forced herself to get out of bed. The sooner she could start packing and get to the airport, the better. Her flight didn't even leave until later this afternoon, but she didn't want to stay in this bed, in this bungalow a moment longer than necessary. She couldn't handle the memories.

The past several days had been the best of her life. Her sister was happily married, her ex was off her back and Mac had set the new standard for any man who would enter her life next. He'd set the bar so high, in fact, she knew no other could ever reach it.

But wasn't the end goal to get Martin to go away? Well, mission accomplished. The cheater wouldn't attempt a reunion now.

As Jenna threw on a sundress and jerked her hair into a ponytail, she almost wished she'd just handled Martin on her own. Then she wouldn't be dealing with this ache in her heart and an overwhelming sense of emptiness.

But how could she regret asking Mac to come here? He'd not only dropped everything to help her, he'd made her feel beautiful and given her a self-confidence she'd never known before.

And it was that confidence that fueled Jenna now. The hurt wasn't going away, but a hefty dose of anger was settling deep alongside it. How dare he leave without a goodbye? Sure, he'd told her they were always going to be friends and, after the scam was up, that's what they would return to. But even friends said goodbye, right? So why had he sneaked out of their bed as if he was ashamed of what they'd done? Could he not face her anymore? Was he in that big of a hurry to get where he was going, to get away from her?

Jenna slammed her suitcase onto the messy bed and started throwing stuff in. She wanted answers and she wanted them now. Texting wasn't going to cut it. She intended to find Mac and demand he tell her why he just left as if she was some cheap date or a one-night stand. She deserved better, damn it.

And isn't that what he'd told her all along?

Mac stormed into the O'Shea family home in Beacon Hill. Braden lived here with Zara. Well, the two went back and forth because neither stubborn party would sell their home. Understandably, Braden didn't want to relinquish what was theirs and Zara didn't want to let go of her late grandmother's house. Thus the stalemate.

The house seemed quiet. Too quiet. No staff? Someone was always milling about during the day.

Mac glanced from room to room and listened for evidence of any activity at all. Upstairs he heard a bedroom door close so Mac made his way up the wide, curved staircase.

When he reached the landing, Braden was heading down the steps. His brother's eyes locked on to Mac's.

"This isn't a good time," Braden murmured as he bounded down the stairs. "I didn't know you were coming."

Stunned at his brother's gruff, put-off tone, Mac watched as Braden passed right by and went down to the first floor. Something was terribly wrong and Mac wasn't leaving until he had answers.

He had zero tolerance for games or for Braden's moodiness. Mac had his own host of issues. Namely the fact he'd fallen for his best friend and now he had to figure out how the hell to keep his distance. Crawling away from her warm body that morning had been one of the hardest things he'd ever done. But as he'd lain there with her body tucked against his, he knew he needed to move on for her own good. He'd seen that look in her eyes, knew that when she'd said "always" she meant it literally. She hadn't just gotten swept away in the moment.

Mac pushed aside the confusion and fear over his emotions and followed Braden into the study on the first floor. Braden circled the oversized mahogany desk and sank into the leather chair behind it. Standing back, Mac watched as Braden rested his elbows on the desktop and held his head in his hands.

Whatever was going on was serious and personal.

"Braden—"

"We lost the baby."

Mac froze. The baby? What…oh, no. Zara had been pregnant? And she'd lost the baby?

With slow, careful steps, Mac approached the desk. No wonder Braden had been out of commission for days. He'd been dealing with a new level of hell.

"I don't know what to do for her," Braden went on. "She's upstairs sleeping now, but she just cries all the time."

Mac rounded the desk and eased a hip on the edge. Looking down at his always strong, always in charge brother and seeing him so broken and miserable was crushing.

"I had no idea, Braden. I'm sorry."

Braden pushed away from the desk and fell back against the cushioned leather. "I didn't want to get into this with a text or phone call. I didn't even know how to cope or to say the words out loud. We'd just found out last week that she was pregnant, and were waiting to get everyone together to make an announcement."

In the span of a week Braden's entire life had changed. Mac completely understood how that worked. Suddenly Mac's issue seemed so insignificant in comparison.

"What can I do?" Mac asked.

Shaking his head, Braden finally met his gaze. "There's nothing. We'll get through this."

Mac had no idea what to say to make any of this easier for Braden. And Zara? He couldn't even imagine what she was going through.

"Tell me what happened with Ryker," Braden said, raking a hand over his face. The stubble beneath his palm rustled. "I hope you took care of whatever he needed."

Mac gritted his teeth and swallowed. Making that judgment call had never come easy, but he couldn't be sorry and he didn't do regrets. Regrets wouldn't change the facts and Mac never believed in looking back.

"We took care of things."

Braden's tired gaze narrowed. "What's that mean?"

Mac came to his feet and paced to the stained-glass window behind the desk. He shoved his hands into his pockets and debated how much he should tell Braden. Normally this would be a nonissue, but given all that Braden was dealing with, Mac worried the news would be too much.

"Ryker has a good lead on the scrolls," Mac started, keeping his back to Braden. "I haven't heard back from him regarding them, so he's still chasing that tip. If it was a dead end, we'd know."

"So what aren't you telling me?"

On a sigh, Mac glanced over his shoulder. "Shane attempted to toss his pathetic power around."

"How?" Braden asked, brows drawn in.

"He intercepted a package that's due for the auction I have coming up in Miami. Nothing we acquired for a client, but he did it to prove he could." Which still pissed Mac off. "He showed up in London and wasn't subtle about following Ryker around."

Braden slammed his hand down on the desk. "He's determined to keep coming at us. Does he think we see him as a threat? Maybe it's time I meet with him face-to-face. Settle this and let him know who exactly is in charge now."

Damn. This was the part he didn't want to tell Braden. "Shane won't be a problem anymore."

Braden's gaze held on to Mac's. Acknowledgment flashed through his eyes, the muscle in his jaw clenched. "Ryker made this call?"

Mac squared his shoulders. "I did."

Braden came to his feet, slowly, lethally. The leather chair creaked, anger rolled off Braden in waves.

"You did."

Mac nodded and fully braced himself for whatever rage Braden threw his way.

In one swift move, Braden gripped Mac's shirt and slammed him against the wall next to the window. "You made this call knowing I didn't want any more death on our hands?" Braden demanded.

"I made the call because we didn't know what was going on with you," Mac gritted out. "I did it because Shane has been a menace since Dad was in charge and I was damn tired of him getting in our way. And he threatened Laney."

The hold on Mac's shirt eased. "He what?"

Mac stared into his brother's eyes, so much like his own. "He sent an email threat to Laney. He tried to encrypt it, but she was able to trace it to him. He also tried to kidnap her."

Braden's eyes narrowed, the muscle in his jaw clenched. "What?"

"He tried to grab her off the street before he went to London to follow Ryker."

"Damn it." Braden's hands fell away, but he didn't move back. "Who the hell attempts to mess with my family and think their actions won't be dealt with?"

Raking his fingers through his hair, he muttered another curse. "That bastard. I should've killed him myself."

A gasp drew Mac's attention. Braden whirled around and in the doorway stood a very pale, very shocked-looking Zara with her hand over her mouth. Her wide eyes were red-rimmed and puffy, a clear sign she'd been crying for a lengthy amount of time.

"Zara…" Braden started across the study.

"Who?" she whispered.

"You should be sleeping," Braden said, ignoring her question.

When he went to reach for her, Zara held up a hand. "Who was killed?"

Braden threw Mac a look over his shoulder. Mac stepped forward. This was his mess, he'd take the blame. "Shane."

Zara's eyes closed, she swayed on her feet and Braden quickly wrapped his arms around her waist and caught her.

"You promised no more."

Mac heard the whispered plea and the guilt consumed him. "The circumstances were different and Braden didn't make the call."

She glanced around Braden and eyed Mac. "But you knew he didn't want anymore…evil. Why did you do it?"

Mac wouldn't feel sorry for making a judgment call. He may hate taking lives, but sometimes there was no other choice…when it meant protecting your own. Just another life lesson from the late Patrick O'Shea.

"I'm sorry about your baby, Zara." He totally ignored her question to him, but he needed her to know he wasn't a complete monster. He was genuinely sorry for the child who was lost. Such innocence taken away. Mac knew how much family meant to Braden, knew his brother wanted a large family of his own.

Her chin quivered, moisture gathered in her eyes as she nodded and leaned farther into Braden.

"We'll talk later," Braden stated, glancing to Mac. "When are you leaving?"

Mac shrugged. "Whenever. My jet is waiting. I need to be home by tomorrow to sort out the last-minute details before the auction."

"Go on, then. Any word from Ryker or anything else business related comes directly to me."

When Braden turned to go, Mac stepped forward. "It was inevitable, you know. Just because you want to take this family in a new direction, doesn't mean you can. Too many outsiders won't let you. They're hiding, waiting to threaten us when we show a hint of weakness. We may want a different life, but change won't be easy."

Braden's shoulders stiffened and he froze for the slightest moment before finally ushering Zara out of the room without a word.

Mac blew out a breath he hadn't even realized he'd been holding. Braden was pissed, Zara was hurt and Jenna was…hell, he didn't know what she was because he'd run out of there the second he realized his feelings had taken a turn in a direction he didn't want to go.

So here he stood in the study of his childhood home,

all alone. In the span of twelve hours he'd managed to anger those closest to him. Now he just needed to throw Ryker and Laney into the mix to round out his crappy day.

Mac pulled out his cell and called his pilot. Might as well get back to Miami and concentrate on work. It was the one area of his life that hadn't fallen spectacularly apart...yet.

Seventeen

All Mac wanted was to crawl into bed and forget the world for a good eight hours. He'd flown from Bora Bora to Boston, then from there he'd come to Miami and gone straight to his new office. After working a few hours, he'd known if he didn't get home, he was going to do a face-plant on his desk.

He needed nothing but his king-sized bed and his phone on silent.

Mac started to unbutton his shirt as he made his way down the hall of his Miami condo. He'd chosen a penthouse with a killer beach view because he was so sick of the unpredictable weather in Boston. Miami was everything he loved: warmth, sunshine and attractive people. The art deco aesthetic in the city was also a great fit for his new offices and auction house. Considering O'Shea's pulled in art with every auction no matter the location, Miami was a no-brainer when it came to opening another branch and Mac had been all too eager to head it up. Not to mention Jenna had planted a bug in his ear about opening an office here since she'd arrived a couple of years back.

His gut clenched at the thought of her. So many times his mind just circled right back around to his best friend and he could do little to control it.

Mac jerked his shirt off and entered his bedroom. Before he could even tap the switch, that familiar floral aroma surrounded him.

"I thought you were never coming home."

Jenna.

Mac quickly flicked the switch, drenching the room in light and his gut clenched at the sight before him. Jenna in his bed. Jenna naked in his bed. Jenna naked in his bed with the sheets rumpled all around her.

She tipped her head to the side and held his gaze.

"I figure you didn't mean to leave me without saying goodbye, so I thought I'd give you that chance," she told him, as if this entire situation didn't warrant any questions.

"How did you know I was coming home?" he asked.

With a shrug, and clearly not concerned with her state of undress, Jenna let the sheets pool at her waist. "I used my key to get in and realized you weren't here. I called Braden, who told me you'd just left."

If he weren't so freaked out about his feelings, about hurting her, he'd be all over her in that bed. Damn, but she was the best accessory in the room.

"You seem to be uncomfortable," she went on. "Everything okay? I mean, I know we said we'd just play this week out, but even friends tell each other goodbye, right? Unless something else was bothering you and that's why you left me. Either way, I deserve an explanation."

Mac remained locked in place. If he took a step forward, he wouldn't be able to control himself. Suddenly sleeping was the last thing he wanted to do in that bed.

"I couldn't stay." At least that was the complete truth.

"Work?" she asked, quirking a brow as if she knew full well that wasn't what caused him to run.

He wadded his shirt up and tossed it toward the basket in the corner. "I can't get into this, Jenna."

As much as he hated to be the guy who was a jerk the morning after, he was going to have to make her leave. She needed to understand exactly what she was dealing with and how far apart their worlds truly were.

"Oh. What exactly can't you get into right now? Would that be your feelings or just the simple courtesy of letting me know you were leaving?"

She was understandably angry and he deserved every bit of backlash she threw his way.

"Are you going to get dressed?" he asked.

Jenna tilted her chin, shot a glare across the room and then slid from the bed. "I suppose now that the week is over you're done. I get it. I was even well aware of the plan going in, but I still thought something had changed."

She let out a laugh, void of any humor, as she scooped up her bra and panties. He watched as she slid into the bright red lingerie that was sure to make any man beg her to crawl back into that bed.

"I figured when you crept out of the room like a coward that you were scared of what had happened, so I was giving you the benefit of the doubt." She reached down and grabbed her red dress, sliding it over her head. "Apparently you felt nothing or you're still freaked out. Either way, I'm not begging. Coming here was a risk I was willing to take, but it looks like only one of us has a set big enough to admit what they want."

As she started to pass, Mac took one step and blocked the doorway. Jenna froze, staring into his eyes. She was clearly pissed, with her lips pressed into a thin line and the muscle ticking in her jaw. But it was the hurt, the vulnerability in her eyes that gutted him. He couldn't let her leave this room thinking she wasn't worth every single thing she wanted.

"I'm man enough to admit what I want, Jenna."

"Prove it."

There was no other way to do this. There was no happy ending between them unless they remained as friends, but was that even an option at this point? Could he honestly look her in the eye and lie about his feelings? He could if he wanted her to forget this notion that the two of them had any type of deeper relationship to build on.

"Wanting you physically has never been the issue," he told her, steeling himself against the fierce determination in her eyes. "But we're done. Not that I wouldn't mind another dose of what you were offering, but let's be honest. We're back home now, reality has settled back in and everything that happened in Bora Bora needs to stay there."

Those gorgeous eyes narrowed and Mac knew he'd struck a nerve, just as he'd intended. The knife he'd used to shred this bond was cutting into him and he was going to hate himself when she walked out of here. But at least she'd be safe, away from his lifestyle, and eventually move on with a man who had a completely legal job. Someone who didn't kill enemies who pissed him off one too many times. Someone who wasn't targeted by dangerous criminals dealing in death.

"You can't lie to me," she stated. "I know you. I know what we had in Bora Bora was real and I know there was something deeper there than just sex."

He said nothing. She was right, but he wasn't about to admit it. He admired her bravery. She'd come so far in such a short amount of time and he couldn't help but feel a swell of pride in knowing he helped her find her self-esteem.

"You can push me away, that's fine," she went on, taking a step back and crossing her arms over her chest. "But you'll be miserable and you'll always wonder what would've happened if you had taken a risk. Isn't that what you O'Sheas do? Take risks?"

She was on fire. The more she talked, the more intense her tone became. She didn't raise her voice, but kept it calm, controlled. Much more lethal that way.

Mac had never been drawn to a meek woman and Jenna LeBlanc was definitely not meek. She was strong, hard-headed, stubborn and determined. He wouldn't expect anything less than a fight because when Jenna wanted something, she went after it. So did he.

"You're more than welcome to stay, but I'm about one minute from falling face-first into bed."

Throwing her arms out to the side, she shook her head and sent him a mock laugh. "Go right ahead. Don't let me get in the way. But remember this, you're the one who let me walk out of here. You're the one who is throwing away something that could be amazing."

Yeah, that was adding salt to the wound. He was fully aware of the life he was throwing away. But the life she wanted, the life she deserved, wasn't the life he could offer her. Constantly keeping secrets, not opening up to her about his work, having to take private calls without her overhearing, would all be too much for a relationship to bear.

"It's for the best." He barely recognized his own voice.

She quirked a brow. "Really? Because you think you're

protecting me? Because you are afraid to fully let me in? Do you think I'm not aware that what your family does isn't completely on the up-and-up? I'm not naive, Mac. Did you ever stop to consider that I'm stronger than you think?"

Shoving his hands in his pockets in an attempt to prevent himself from touching her, Mac nodded. "I'm fully aware how strong you are, Jenna. You're one of the strongest people I know. But anything between us beyond friendship isn't possible."

"You think we can just return to being friends now?" Her eyes held his as if she truly thought he had a simple answer for such a complex question.

"That's our only option. You'll find someone you love and you'll spend the rest of your life with him. You'll wear your mother's wedding dress and get that fairy tale you want."

"You think that's what this is? Me looking for some fairy tale?" Jenna turned, paced his bedroom. "I didn't get swept into the moment on the island, Mac. I spent more time with you, I got to know more of you and I opened more of myself to you than I ever had before."

"Which will only make our friendship stronger," he stated, as if that justified her deep connection and let him off the hook from feeling any more for her.

Standing here before her, he knew full well he was being a jerk, but he literally saw no other way out of this. Making her unhappy now would help simplify her life and make her happier in the long run. He had to remain detached from that longing look in her eyes, that questioning stare full of the hope that he was shattering.

"This is ridiculous." Jenna shook her head and started for the door again. "Move."

Mac remained still. She glanced down to the floor, then back up, blinking against the unshed tears in her eyes.

Enough. Mac snapped and grabbed her arms, hauling her against his chest. He ignored her shocked gasp.

"You think this is ridiculous?" he demanded with a slight shake. "What's ridiculous is thinking a relationship can work between us. You need to trust me on this, Jenna. I'm pushing you away because I care about you, not because I don't want more."

Her eyes roamed his face as she blinked, taking in his statement. "You want more? As in…what?"

No. He wasn't taking the bait. Discussing things that could never happen was moot.

"It doesn't matter," he claimed. "What matters is our friendship. I need to keep you at a distance, to prevent you from getting in too deep. This way you're still in my life and you can have your own life without the stress that comes from living in mine."

"And you're making this decision for me?" she asked, quirking a brow.

He pushed her back and raked a hand through his hair. "Yes, damn it."

Jenna's mocking laugh had his gut clenching. She still didn't see that he was doing all of this because he cared so much…too much. And this was why he didn't do relationships. Too many ways to get hurt, both physically and emotionally. He wished she would see that remaining friends was their best option.

His cell vibrated in his pocket, but he ignored it for the time being. He'd check it once Jenna was gone.

"I'm not sure friendship is an area I want to go with you again," she told him, her defiant little chin lifted. "I've seen how much you care for me. I know it's in there and the fact that you're ignoring it only tells me how much you love me."

Mac jerked back. "I never said love."

In that moment a veil seemed to cover her face. Jenna's lips thinned, her lids lowered slightly as she gave a brief nod.

"That's all I needed to know. I'm sorry I made a fool of—"

"Hold on." He jerked the vibrating phone from his pocket. "I have to take this. Don't leave."

Her eyes widened as if she couldn't believe he'd cut her off.

The screen flashed Ryker's name.

"Hey, man."

"How soon can you meet me in London?" Ryker asked.

Mac's eyes darted to Jenna. "Did you find something?"

"I believe so. I called Braden and he said to see if you could come. He told me about Zara."

Mac swallowed his remorse. He hadn't told Jenna, hadn't wanted to pull the sympathy card.

With his eyes locked on Jenna, Mac replied, "I'll call my pilot and be in the air within the hour."

Mac listened as Ryker went on to explain where he was staying and how hopeful he was that this was the lead they'd been waiting for.

But all the while, Jenna was grabbing her purse from the dresser, pulling out her keys and brushing by him without a word or even a glance in his direction.

Before he could finish the call with Ryker, his front door opened and shut with an echoing click. He'd gotten his wish. He'd pushed her away and now Ryker had a lead on the scrolls the O'Sheas had been in search of for decades.

Now that everything seemed to be within his grasp, now that he was ready to go after his father's legacy, why did he feel such a void? Why did he have a gut-sinking feeling that the very best thing that would ever happen to him had just walked out that door? And she'd walked out because he'd told her to; he'd forced her hand and left her no choice.

No regrets. Isn't that the motto he'd always lived by?

For the first time in his life, Mac was second-guessing every action, every choice he'd made for the past week and wondering how the control had slipped from his grasp. Then he realized Jenna had always been the one with the control. As much as he thought himself so powerful and strong, Jenna was the force behind all of that.

Sliding the cell back into his pocket, the fact he hadn't slept for over a day didn't even register. All he knew was that as soon as he got back from London, as soon as this auction in Miami was wrapped up next week, he was focusing on Jenna. Somehow, he had to make this right.

Now he had to figure out exactly what he wanted from her because he couldn't keep hurting her. Their friendship was over, no doubt about that. Now he either needed to cut ties completely or fully submerge her in his world, where he could protect her and keep her safe from his enemies.

Mac grabbed his bag by the door and quickly exchanged some of his clothes as he rang his pilot. When he ended the call, his eyes went to the rumpled bed and he couldn't forget that image of coming home and seeing Jenna in his bed.

Just that act alone spoke volumes about the woman she'd become since last week. A woman he'd seen come out of her shell, a woman who willingly gave him everything he'd ever wanted and stood up to him. She'd shown no fear, had looked him full in the face and called him a coward. There wasn't a soul on Earth who had ever done that.

Which proved Jenna LeBlanc may just be the dynamic woman he'd never known he was looking for. He'd kept secrets from her for years, had kept his business separate from his personal life and she'd never questioned him. So how would being fully involved with her be any different?

A thread of hope slid through him at the possibilities. He had a few surprises in store for Jenna. In the end, he knew there was only one choice to make. There was no way he'd let her walk away from him again.

Eighteen

"Well, that went better than we hoped."

Mac sank into a vacant chair. The auction was over and the sales had been record-breaking. He considered this a good sign of things to come in Miami.

Too bad nothing had come of the whirlwind trip to London. In addition, the incident Mac had ordered Ryker to take care of was over and done. Braden hadn't said another word, but Mac was well aware of his brother's stance. There would be no more killings. They would have to find another way to protect their own.

Braden took a seat next to Mac and slapped his back. "You pulled it off. Dad would be proud."

Mac swallowed a lump of regret. That's what he wanted. He missed his dad, wanted him to be proud of the way he'd taken their business into another territory.

"I sent Zara to the condo to get some rest," Braden went on. "She was worn out."

Once Mac had opened a branch in Miami, Braden went ahead and bought a condo to have for visits. Smart move. Zara had looked dead on her feet. She was taking this miscarriage hard.

"How are you guys doing?" Mac asked.

With a shrug, Braden stared straight ahead to the now-empty stage. "We're getting better each day. As soon as the doctor says it's safe, we'll try again."

"I said I'm fine to drive," snapped a familiar voice.

Braden let out a sigh that matched Mac's. "Here we go again," Braden muttered.

Mac glanced over his shoulder to see Laney storming down the aisle, Ryker hot on her heels. Literally. The woman insisted on wearing sky-high shoes to every damn event.

"Tell the family bouncer that I'm fine to drive."

Mac nearly laughed at her childish attitude, complete with crossed arms and tapping foot, but he rather liked not having his head bitten off.

"She received another threat," Ryker stated in that low, controlled tone of his. "She won't tell you because she doesn't want anyone to worry."

"And if you hadn't been snooping in my things, you wouldn't know, either," Laney bit out.

Braden came to his feet. "What the hell is this about another threat? Who is it now?"

Mercy, would the threats ever end? Shouldn't taking their family in a safer direction ensure that those he loved would be secure?

What about Jenna? No matter the cost, he had to keep her safe. She was associated with his family and therefore automatically a mark.

Laney shrugged. "I don't know who this one came from and I'm not concerned. Just some hacker causing a slight problem. Nothing I can't handle and nothing like Shane."

Mac scrounged up the last bit of energy he had. "Let Ryker see you back to your condo. There's no reason not to."

"I'm a big girl," she said through gritted teeth. "Would you ask Ryker to hold your hand if someone threatened you?"

Mac and Braden exchanged a look. Ryker remained silent, shoving his hands in his pockets, but keeping his eyes on Laney.

"That's what I thought," she said. "I'm going back to my condo. Alone. I will gladly text each of you once I arrive so you know the big bad wolf didn't get me."

She leaned past Mac and hugged Braden. "Love you. Tell Zara I'll call her tomorrow and take her out for some girl time."

"She'd like that," Braden replied.

When Laney hugged Mac, he squeezed her back and said, "Don't be stubborn. Let him take you."

Laney eased back and smiled. "Good night, big brother."

She turned, squaring her shoulders and glaring at Ryker. "Your concern is noted, but not necessary. Good night."

And like the regal woman their mother always was, Laney took a chapter from Elizabeth O'Shea's book and walked out with head high and back straight.

Mac shot Ryker a look.

"I'm on it."

Ryker kept his distance, but slowly followed Laney out the door.

"Those two may end up in a fistfight before the night is over," Braden commented.

"Ryker's good, but my vote is on Laney. Mainly because she's pissed and Ryker would never hurt a woman."

"What about you?" Braden asked, leaning against the back of one plush chair. "You have dodged any topics concerning Jenna and I thought for sure she'd be here on your big night."

Mac snorted. "Don't ask."

"Let me focus on your problems for a while," Braden said. "We've had a successful night, Zara's resting and it's just you and me. Lay it on me."

Mac found himself pouring out the details of the last two weeks as if he were some damn woman chatting with her friends. But he needed Braden's advice and he was more than willing to offer his brother a distraction.

"So you pretended to be engaged and now…what? You want to actually be engaged?"

Mac raked a hand through his hair. "Hell, I don't know what I want. I know I want her back and as more than a friend, but to take it that far… I don't know."

"And you haven't seen her in a week?"

Mac shook his head. Not since he'd been on the phone with Ryker and she'd looked at him like he was a monster. He'd never get that image out of his head. He'd chosen work over her and he'd quite possibly destroyed her.

"I thought I'd have everything figured out by now, but it's been a week and I still don't know how to approach her."

Braden laughed. "On your knees, buddy. Plan on doing a lot of groveling. I've been there. It's hell on the ego and pride, but well worth it in the end."

Mac knew Jenna would be worth everything, but was he willing to risk her happiness for his selfish need to be with her? Would she get tired of all the secrets, all the

sneaking around and him unable to answer the questions
she was bound to have?

The scrolls were still out there somewhere and it tore
him up that he had so little control over getting them
back. But there was one thing that was still very much
in his hands.

He was ready to fight for his girl.

Jenna rolled over in bed and froze. Why did she smell
her mango tea? There was another scent that filtered in
as well...some pastry? What?

Jenna jerked up in bed. She lived alone so any smell
coming from the other room was a bit alarming.

She tossed the covers aside and tiptoed to the doorway. She opened the crack wider to peer out. From just
the right angle she could see into the kitchen and what
she saw stopped her cold.

Mac. He was bustling around in her kitchen as if he
owned the place. She should've taken his key back the
day she'd surprised him at his place, but she'd been too
hurt and too angry. All she'd wanted to do was get out
of his sight before she broke down and he saw exactly
how much he affected her.

So after a week of nothing, what was he doing here?

Whatever it was, she wasn't going to give him an inch.
She turned and headed into her master bath and went
about her daily routine. She washed her face, pulled her
hair back and brushed her teeth. Since this was Sunday,
the flower shop was closed and she usually cleaned. But
even if Mac weren't in the other room she still wouldn't
feel like it.

In the past two weeks she'd gone from a beautiful state
of euphoria to the lowest level of depression she could
remember. No matter what she did, she was reminded of

Mac. They just had too many memories together. Movies, food, random little shops near her condo, countless places that held a piece of them, and she couldn't function.

How pathetic did that sound? Well, she could function, but she didn't want to. She wasn't quite finished with her moping just yet. He'd hurt her, hurt her badly, and she wondered if she'd every truly get over it.

In Bora Bora he'd been demanding, exhilarating and positively perfect. Then she'd seen him mask his feelings, hide behind work and force her to walk away. She wouldn't beg. She had too much respect for herself to ask a man to stick around. Mac may have wanted to ignore his feelings, but she wished he'd just come clean.

Which made her wonder, was that why he'd let himself in this morning? He was the only other person who knew her passcode for the security alarm, so he'd been quite stealthy about it.

But if he was in there making her breakfast, the least she could do was hear what he had to say. Then she'd have to decide what to do.

Perhaps he was just here because he thought they could get back to friend status. If that was the case, Jenna wasn't so sure she could handle that deal. She'd gotten too close to the man she wanted in her life forever. She'd seen a glimpse of the man who cared for her the way she deserved to be, and Jenna knew he loved her. He may not have admitted it to himself, but he did.

Her heart tumbled in her chest as she exited her bathroom and glanced down at her silky chemise. He'd seen her completely naked, so changing would be ridiculous. Besides, Mac was the only man she'd ever wanted to bare it all to. He made her feel beautiful and he showed her that she was sexy with curves, dips and a little extra weight.

And if he was here for the whole "let's be friends" spiel, maybe her state of dress—or undress—would make him suffer just a bit more.

Pulling in a deep breath, Jenna opened her bedroom door and padded down the tiled hallway. She stood in the open entryway to the kitchen and propped a hand on her hip. Or should she cross her arms? Maybe place both hands on her hips?

Jenna groaned inwardly. Maybe coming out here half naked wasn't the best option. It's not as if she had this whole seductress thing down, and why was she even trying? She wasn't the one who should be putting forth the effort now…right?

Rolling her eyes at herself, she started to turn when Mac glanced over his shoulder and his heavy-lidded, intense look froze her in place. So much emotion shone through those eyes: regret, desire, vulnerability.

"What are you doing here?" she asked, surprised her voice sounded stronger than she was actually feeling.

"Making your favorite breakfast."

She quirked a brow and slid her gaze to the box on the counter from their favorite bakery down the street. "Really?"

"I made mango tea to go with your Danish."

He turned around and leaned back against the counter, blocking the plate she'd gotten a glimpse of. His eyes raked over her body, and the effect was just as potent as if he'd touched her with his bare hands. But she didn't move any closer. She would keep her distance until she knew the full meaning of his visit. Her favorite breakfast was a nice start, though.

"I've missed you."

Jenna stilled, her breath catching in her throat. "Is that why I haven't seen or heard from you in a week?"

"I had to sort some things out. I was hoping you'd be at the auction."

Jenna lifted a shoulder. "I was hoping you wouldn't hurt me on purpose. I guess we're even."

Okay, that was petty, but damn it, she'd never been in this position before. She had no clue what the rules were when your heart was beaten and bruised.

"I'm sorry." Those bright eyes held her in place as the sincere apology wrapped around her. "I went about everything the wrong way."

Jenna crossed her arms. "Yes, you did."

A smile flirted around Mac's mouth. "You're not going to make this easy, are you?"

"Should I?"

"I wouldn't expect any less from the woman I love."

Taken aback by the sudden declaration, Jenna reached for the doorframe to steady herself. "What?"

"I love you," he announced, as if he'd said the words a million times before and was utterly comfortable with them. "As more than a friend. I wanted to keep you at arm's length, to keep you away from the ugliness that can sometimes surround my family."

Pulling her thoughts back together, Jenna stepped forward and gripped the back of a barstool at the center island. "We've danced around the topic for years now. I'm not judging you. I'm already in your life, so why not let me in a bit deeper?"

His gaze darted to the floor as he shook his head. With a heavy sigh, he glanced back to her. "I don't know how to answer that. I guess I thought keeping you as a friend but nothing more would be the best way to protect you. I could still have you in my life, but..."

Mac pushed off the counter and started pacing. Resembling a caged animal, he made a couple of laps before stopping on the other side of the island. He rested his palms on the countertop and let his head drop.

"I don't even know how to do this, Jen."

The brokenness in his tone nearly undid her, but she had to remain strong. Whatever internal battle he waged with himself was fierce. He needed to work through this in order to move forward. She desperately wanted to move forward with him and she hoped that was why he was here.

"I've done things," he whispered. "Things I never want you to know about. Not because I don't trust you, but because I don't want you to look at me with fear or hate."

Jenna gripped the back of the stool. "I would never look at you that way."

His eyes drilled into hers. "You did when you walked out last week."

Swallowing, Jenna pulled up every ounce of strength she could muster and circled the island. "I didn't fear or hate you, Mac. Never. I was disappointed, hurt and frustrated. I know the loyalty you have to your family and I admire you for it. I know there will be times you'll choose the business over me and I get that, too. But you were pushing me away, and to drive the point home you didn't even offer a goodbye. I was just like all the other women in your life and I won't be treated like that."

Mac reached for her, finally. His fingers curled around her bare arms. Jenna pulled in a deep breath, the tips of her breasts brushing against his T-shirt.

"You'll never be treated like just any other woman, Jenna. You're nothing like anyone I've ever been with before."

"Tell me again," she whispered, emotions clogging her throat. "Tell me you love me."

His hands slid down her sides and gripped her waist.

The strength of his touch warmed her entire body through the silk.

"I'd rather show you," he muttered against her lips. "But I do love you, Jenna. So much. More than I ever thought possible."

Wrapping her arms around him, she nipped at his lips. As if that set off some sort of spark in him, Mac lifted her up against him. Instinctively her legs went around his waist as he carried her from the room. She kissed his stubbled jawline as he made his way toward her bedroom.

"I need you now," he growled as they toppled onto the bed.

In a frenzy, he tore his clothes off and yanked her chemise down. Poised above her, he stared into her eyes. "Nothing between us," he told her.

Jenna nodded. She never wanted anything between them again. When Mac joined their bodies, Jenna wrapped herself around him, taking in all of his strength. This is what they were, a team, a force. They were lovers, best friends and so much more.

Mac's lips moved over hers, then down her throat as she arched into his touch. He whispered her name as she climbed and when she flew apart, he told her once again how much he loved her and then followed her over the edge.

Moments later, Jenna lay tucked against his side. There was so much that still needed to be said, so much that needed to be hashed out, but right now, she had all she needed.

When her stomach growled, she snuggled a bit deeper. "I'm starving. I worked up an appetite."

Mac slid his hand up her back and into her hair, which had fallen from the ponytail. "Stay here and I'll bring you breakfast."

When he got up, Jenna admired his perfect male form. And he was all hers.

"Look at me like that and I'll never make it out of this room," he told her.

"Bring me breakfast and I'll thank you properly."

He closed his eyes and groaned. "You're killing me. Don't move."

Moments later he had her tea and a plate of Danishes in hand.

"I'm pretty sure I could never get tired of you serving me breakfast in bed while naked."

He smiled as he placed the items on her bedside table. Mac sank down beside her, caging her in as he put a hand on either side of her hips. "Then marry me and I'll do this every day."

Jenna gasped. "What?"

"Marry me, Jenna. I don't want to be your fake fiancé or your pretend lover. I want it all."

Her mind spun in circles. Were they ready for this?

"Marriage is a big leap, Mac. Aren't we moving too fast?"

He laughed and smacked her lips with a kiss. "I've wanted you for years, Jen. I want to wake up with you every single morning and I want you to be legally mine. I can't get a ring on your finger fast enough."

Tears pricked her eyes. "Mac," she whispered.

"Before you say yes, I need to know something."

Blinking against the moisture, Jenna nodded. "Anything."

"Do you love me?"

Her heart swelled. As if there was ever any doubt as to her feelings, she threw her arms around his neck and kissed him. "I love you more than anything in this world.

I don't care what you do, I know you'll always keep me safe. I will marry you today, tomorrow, whenever."

He folded her into his chest and sighed against her neck. "I want you to have the wedding you've always dreamed of. I want you to wear your mother's dress."

Jenna smiled and pulled back. "I guess we can officially tell them we're getting married now?"

"Did they ever know any different?" he asked.

"No."

Mac shrugged. "Then let's not tell them. We're only moving forward. No regrets and no looking back."

"I couldn't agree more." She trailed her fingertip along the coarse hair covering his jaw. "But I want a honeymoon in Bora Bora."

"I want a honeymoon for the rest of our lives all over the world."

Mac laid Jenna back on the bed and proceeded to get started on that honeymoon…breakfast forgotten once again.

Epilogue

"We have a problem."

Words Mac never liked to hear, especially from Braden. They'd been riding life too easily lately...well, easily for them. Of course something had to land in their laps.

"What?" he asked, gripping the phone.

Jenna had gone shopping with her mother. Only a week ago he'd officially asked her to marry him and now the women were out planning. Mac didn't care what she planned, so long as she was his wife sooner rather than later.

"Laney called and said she's come across some chatter of an investigation being done on the down low."

"And we're the subject?"

"Yeah."

Damn it. "Do we know where the threat is coming from?" Mac asked, sinking into his leather office chair.

"Not yet. She just called me, but she's trying to hack into more databases," Braden explained. "She said this will take some time, so we need to keep things squeaky clean until we know where the real danger is."

Mac rested his elbows on his desk and eyed his shut door. He'd come into the office early but kept the door shut because he hadn't wanted to be disturbed when his assistant came in.

"Do you think it's someone who works for us or some unknown entity trying to get close to us?"

Braden blew out a frustrated breath. "I have no idea and I'm pissed. We don't know who set this into motion or how many are involved."

"We need to figure out who it is as soon as possible. We can't alert our allies in the FBI or local law enforcement until we know what we're up against."

"Trust me, Laney is on it and she's just as pissed as we are. Nobody comes at us like this."

And lives, Mac wanted to say. But he wasn't going to get into that hot debate again. As much as Braden wanted to move their family into a new, less violent territory, there had to be repercussions for such actions.

Still, it was a topic they could and would discuss once they knew more details.

"Does Ryker know?"

"I'm calling him next," Braden explained. "Just keep Jenna close until we know what we're up against. This may be someone out to harm us physically or attack our business. Damn it, I hate being in the dark."

Mac swallowed. This was one of the reasons he'd hesitated letting Jenna in so deep. But he realized that having her close was the best place for her. It was the only way to ensure her safety.

"I'll be sure to stay on high alert. We just need to keep Ryker in the background for now. Even the scroll hunt needs to be suspended. If he discovered where they were and went in—"

"Yeah. I know. I'll make sure he understands the severity of the situation."

"Any other bad news?" Mac asked.

"That's it. But I want you to be watching everything in your offices. This timing reeks and I don't believe in coincidences. We didn't have an issue until we opted to open new branches and I'm wondering if there's a plant in either the Miami or Atlanta location."

Mac came to his feet and rubbed the back of his neck. "I'll have Laney look deeper into the new employees' personal lives. I want texts, where they go on their time off, everything."

"Good idea."

Mac wondered if this would be too much to put on their sister, but she was just as strong and resilient as the rest of them…a point she often reminded them of. Still, she was their baby sister and they felt the need to shelter her.

"I need to get ahold of Ryker."

Mac stood at his floor-to-ceiling office windows and stared out onto the city. "I'll keep you posted if anything turns up."

Just as he disconnected the call, his office door flew open. Mac jerked in defense, but relaxed when he saw Jenna in the doorway loaded down with bags.

"I did some damage," she said as she breezed in. "Mom dropped me off on her way to the salon. I booked her an appointment and…what's wrong?"

She dumped the bags into the leather club chair by the

door and crossed to him. "Mac?" she asked, her brows drawn in.

He wrapped an arm around her and kissed the top of her head. "Nothing."

Jenna pulled back, her hand on his chest. "We're a team now, remember? If you can't give me details, I understand, but don't lie to my face."

"There's been a threat to the family. I don't know if it's personal or business. I really have no details but I can tell you that you're safe. I just need you to be vigilant when you're not with me."

She studied his face. "I know you'll protect me, but what about you? Who's going to protect you?"

"I'm fine." He squeezed her tighter against him as he stared out the window. "Everything will be fine, Jenna. I swear to you."

And that was a promise he'd never break. Regardless of his family's new direction, if anyone ever posed a threat to what belonged to Mac, he'd personally see to destroying that person with his bare hands.

"You believe you're safe, right? Promise me you're not going to worry about this."

Jenna looked up into his eyes. "I'm not worried one bit. I know you wouldn't lie to me about that."

"I love you, Jenna."

A smile spread across her face. "I love you. More than anything. Shall I lock the door and give you a sneak peek at what I purchased for our honeymoon?"

Arousal slammed into him. "Is that a rhetorical question?"

As he watched his fiancée close and lock the door, he knew he'd die before letting anything happen to her. This was the start of their life together and things may be rocky, but for now, having Jenna do some insanely erotic striptease in his office was all he needed. She was all he needed and they would face anything in the outside world together.

* * * * *

If you liked this novel, check out the first book in the **MAFIA MOGULS** *series from Jules Bennett:*

TRAPPED WITH THE TYCOON

And pick up these other emotional and sexy reads from Jules Bennett:

BEHIND PALACE DOORS
WHAT THE PRINCE WANTS
A ROYAL AMNESIA SCANDAL
WHEN OPPOSITES ATTRACT...

All available now, only from Harlequin Desire!

If you're on Twitter, tell us what you think of Harlequin Desire! #harlequindesire

COMING NEXT MONTH FROM

HARLEQUIN® *Desire*

Available June 7, 2016

#2449 REDEEMING THE BILLIONAIRE SEAL
Billionaires and Babies • by Lauren Canan
Navy SEAL Chance Masters is only back on the family ranch until his next deployment, but can the all-grown-up girl next door struggling to raise her infant niece convince him his rightful place is at home?

#2450 A BRIDE FOR THE BOSS
Texas Cattleman's Club: Lies and Lullabies
by Maureen Child
When Mac's overworked assistant quits, he's left floundering. But when she challenges the wealthy rancher to spend two weeks not working—with *her*—he soon realizes all the pleasures he's been missing...

#2451 A PREGNANCY SCANDAL
Love and Lipstick • by Kat Cantrell
One broken rule. One night of passion. Now...one accidental pregnancy! A marriage of convenience is the only way to prevent a scandal for the popular senator and his no-frills CFO lover—until their union becomes so much more...

#2452 THE BOSS AND HIS COWGIRL
Red Dirt Royalty • by Silver James
Clay Barron is an oil magnate bred for great things. Nothing can stop his ambition—except the beautiful assistant from his hometown. Will his craving for the former cowgirl mean a choice between love and success?

#2453 ARRANGED MARRIAGE, BEDROOM SECRETS
Courtesan Brides • by Yvonne Lindsay
To prepare for his arranged marriage, Prince Thierry hires a mysterious beauty to tutor him in romance. His betrothed, Mila, mischievously takes the woman's place. But as the prince falls for his "forbidden" lover, Mila's revelations will threaten all they hold dear...

#2454 TRAPPED WITH THE MAVERICK MILLIONAIRE
From Mavericks to Married • by Joss Wood
Years ago, one kiss from a hockey superstar rocked Rory's world. Now Mac needs her—as his live-in physical therapist! Despite their explosive chemistry, she keeps her hands off—until one hot island night as a storm rages...

REQUEST YOUR FREE BOOKS!
2 FREE NOVELS PLUS 2 FREE GIFTS!

HARLEQUIN®

Desire

ALWAYS POWERFUL, PASSIONATE AND PROVOCATIVE

YES! Please send me 2 FREE Harlequin® Desire novels and my 2 FREE gifts (gifts are worth about $10). After receiving them, if I don't wish to receive any more books, I can return the shipping statement marked "cancel." If I don't cancel, I will receive 6 brand-new novels every month and be billed just $4.55 per book in the U.S. or $5.24 per book in Canada. That's a savings of at least 13% off the cover price! It's quite a bargain! Shipping and handling is just 50¢ per book in the U.S. and 75¢ per book in Canada.* I understand that accepting the 2 free books and gifts places me under no obligation to buy anything. I can always return a shipment and cancel at any time. Even if I never buy another book, the two free books and gifts are mine to keep forever.

225/326 HDN GH2P

Name	(PLEASE PRINT)

Address	Apt. #

City	State/Prov.	Zip/Postal Code

Signature (if under 18, a parent or guardian must sign)

Mail to the **Reader Service:**

IN U.S.A.: P.O. Box 1867, Buffalo, NY 14240-1867
IN CANADA: P.O. Box 609, Fort Erie, Ontario L2A 5X3

Want to try two free books from another line?
Call 1-800-873-8635 or visit www.ReaderService.com.

* Terms and prices subject to change without notice. Prices do not include applicable taxes. Sales tax applicable in N.Y. Canadian residents will be charged applicable taxes. Offer not valid in Quebec. This offer is limited to one order per household. Not valid for current subscribers to Harlequin Desire books. All orders subject to credit approval. Credit or debit balances in a customer's account(s) may be offset by any other outstanding balance owed by or to the customer. Please allow 4 to 6 weeks for delivery. Offer available while quantities last.

Your Privacy—The Reader Service is committed to protecting your privacy. Our Privacy Policy is available online at www.ReaderService.com or upon request from the Reader Service.

We make a portion of our mailing list available to reputable third parties that offer products we believe may interest you. If you prefer that we not exchange your name with third parties, or if you wish to clarify or modify your communication preferences, please visit us at www.ReaderService.com/consumerchoice or write to us at Reader Service Preference Service, P.O. Box 9062, Buffalo, NY 14240-9062. Include your complete name and address.

HDI5

It had been a long day, but a good one.

Andi was feeling pretty smug about her decision to
quit her job and deliberately ignoring the occasional
twinges of regret. She should have done it three years
ago. As soon as she realized she was in love with a man
who would never see her as more than a piece of office
equipment.

Her heart ached a little, but she took another sip of
wine and purposefully drowned that pain. Once she was
free of her idle daydreams of Mac, she'd be able to look
around, find a man to be with. To help her build the life
she wanted so badly.

Her arms ached from wielding a paint roller, but
working on her home felt good. So good, in fact, she didn't
even grumble when someone knocked on the front door.

Wineglass in hand, she answered the door and jolted when Mac smiled at her.

"Mac? What're you doing here?"

"Hello to you, too," he said and stepped past her, unasked, into the house.

All she could do was close the door and follow him into the living room.

He turned around and gave her a quick smile that had her stomach jittering in response before she could quash her automatic response. "The color's good."

"Thanks. Mac, why are you here?"

"I'm here because I wanted to get a look at what you left me for." His gaze fixed on her and for the first time, he noticed that she wore a tiny tank top and a silky pair of drawstring pants. Her feet were bare and her toenails were painted a soft blush pink. Her hair was long and loose over her shoulders, just skimming the tops of her breasts.

Mac took a breath and wondered where that flash of heat had come from. He'd been with Andi nearly every day for the past six years and he'd never reacted to her like this before.

Now it seemed to be all he could notice.

Whatever You're Into… Passionate Reads

Looking for more passionate reads from Harlequin®?
Fear not! Harlequin® Presents, Harlequin® Desire and
Harlequin® Blaze offer you irresistible romance stories
featuring powerful heroes.

◆HARLEQUIN *Presents.*

Do you want alpha males, decadent glamour and jet-set
lifestyles? Step into the sensational, sophisticated world of
Harlequin® Presents, where sinfully tempting heroes ignite a
fierce and wickedly irresistible passion!

◆HARLEQUIN *Desire*

Harlequin® Desire novels are powerful, passionate and
provocative contemporary romances set against a backdrop of
wealth, privilege and sweeping family saga. Alpha heroes with
a soft side meet strong-willed but vulnerable heroines amid a
dramatic world of divided loyalties, high-stakes conflict and
intense emotion.

◆HARLEQUIN *Blaze*

Harlequin® Blaze stories sizzle with strong heroines and
irresistible heroes playing the game of modern love and lust.
They're fun, sexy and always steamy.

Be sure to check out our full selection of books
within each series every month!

www.Harlequin.com